SPIES IN PLAIN SIGHT

Also by Lynn Hightower

The Junie Lagarde novels

THE BEAUTIFUL RISK *

The Enlightenment Project novels

THE ENLIGHTENMENT PROJECT *
THE HUNTING DARK *

Novels

HIGH WATER
THE PIPER *
EVEN IN DARKNESS *

The Sonora Blair series

EYESHOT
FLASHPOINT
NO GOOD DEED
THE DEBT COLLECTOR

The David Silver series

ALIEN BLUES
ALIEN EYES
ALIEN HEAT
ALIEN RITES

The Lena Padget series

SATAN'S LAMBS
FORTUNES OF THE DEAD
WHEN SECRETS DIE

*available from Severn House

SPIES IN PLAIN SIGHT

Lynn Hightower

SEVERN HOUSE

First world edition published in Great Britain and the USA in 2025
by Severn House, an imprint of Canongate Books Ltd,
14 High Street, Edinburgh EH1 1TE.

severnhouse.com

Copyright © Lynn Hightower, 2025

Cover and jacket design by Jem Butcher Design

All rights reserved including the right of reproduction in whole or in part in any form. The right of Lynn Hightower to be identified as the author of this work has been asserted in accordance with the Copyright, Designs & Patents Act 1988.

British Library Cataloguing-in-Publication Data
A CIP catalogue record for this title is available from the British Library.

ISBN-13: 978-1-4483-1398-3 (cased)
ISBN-13: 978-1-4483-1399-0 (e-book)

This is a work of fiction. Names, characters, places and incidents are either the product of the author's imagination or are used fictitiously. Except where actual historical events and characters are being described for the storyline of this novel, all situations in this publication are fictitious and any resemblance to actual persons, living or dead, business establishments, events or locales is purely coincidental.

No part of this book may be used or reproduced in any manner for the purpose of training artificial intelligence technologies or systems. This work is reserved from text and data mining (Article 4(3) Directive (EU) 2019/790).

All Severn House titles are printed on acid-free paper.

Typeset by Palimpsest Book Production Ltd., Falkirk, Stirlingshire, Scotland.
Printed and bound in Great Britain by TJ Books, Padstow, Cornwall.

The manufacturer's authorised representative in the EU for product safety is Authorised Rep Compliance Ltd, 71 Lower Baggot Street, Dublin D02 P593 Ireland (arccompliance.com)

Praise for Lynn Hightower

"A gripping, suspenseful read"
Booklist on *The Beautiful Risk*

"Dark and swiftly moving, both a thriller and an examination of how deep a connection can be"
Kirkus Reviews on *The Beautiful Risk*

"Sensitive characterizations match the imaginative plot. Readers will compulsively turn the pages to see how it all ends"
Publishers Weekly Starred Review of
The Enlightenment Project

"Lynn Hightower is a brave, bold writer . . . Super-recommended!"
Lee Child on *The Enlightenment Project*

"This taut psychological page-turner has a gripping, tightly woven plot and is jam-packed with head-spinning twists . . . Will keep readers riveted"
Booklist on *Even in Darkness*

"Compelling"
Kirkus Reviews on *Even in Darkness*

About the author

Lynn Hightower is the internationally bestselling author of numerous thriller and horror novels, including the Sonora Blair and Lena Padget detective series, the Enlightenment Project supernatural suspense series and the Junie Lagard novels. Her novels have been included in the *New York Times*' list of Notable Books and *The Times*' bestseller lists, and she has won the Shamus Award for Best First Private Eye novel and a WHSmith Fresh Talent Award. Lynn shares her office with her German Shepherd, Leah, and spends as much time as possible in France.

www.lynnhightower.com

For Robert. Demain c'est toi.

Acknowledgments

My thanks to Patrice Rayssac, for insights on French culture, and introducing me to the musical inspiration for the book, the song 'Je veux' by Zaz. Alessia De Paola for cheering my outrageous plot twists, in novels and real life. Carl and Jenn Moses, for encouragement and character therapy. Rachel Slatter, Editorial Director of Severn House, for insights on structure and storytelling, and Martin Brown, Senior Brand Manager of Severn House, for marketing savvy. Matt Bialer, Bailey Tomayo and Dorothy Vincent at Sanford J. Greenburger. Marla Carleton and Axel Meunch of Specto Design for brilliant ad campaigns and creating an award-winning website. *You guys.*

For gatherings over good food and holidays with all of my beautiful babies, grown and little. And my muse, bodyguard, and hearing assistance German Shepherd, Leah. Thank you for walkies and matching your steps to mine when I needed it most.

A bon chat, bon rat. –To a good cat, a good rat.

Let go of your Daddy's musty, fusty, dusty espionage and welcome to VIE. A spy organization of the people, by the people, and for the people. *We are spies in plain sight.* We make billionaires afraid.

ONE

Three minutes before it all began, there was a touch of grace, a golden moment. An awareness of what the French call dépaysement – a feeling that I was far from home but exactly where I was meant to be. It brought a rush of quiet joy as I drifted down the rain-washed Rue Sainte-Claire in Annecy, France – the city that owns my heart. Heading for Cafe de la Place, where I would sit outside and have a morning coffee, look at the fountain, and think of hopefully nothing at all.

Two minutes before it all began, I had a jolt of intuition. A sure but mysterious knowledge of upheaval, the world beneath my feet rippling and buckling. And where it would settle – and *if* it would settle – I could not know. *Something* was coming for me.

The early-morning sounds of the city, footsteps, a snatch of conversation. All of it receded like the tide going out, and I had that flood of energy that becomes awareness. A glimpse of life in the real, before I became distracted, yet again, by the dream.

One minute before it all began, I caught a glimpse of him, Charl St Priest. I thought it was a trick of the light – but no. It was him. Long dead but looking like flesh and blood, head shattered by the bullet I had fired into his left temple.

A man who had envied and loathed my beloved husband, Olivier. Who killed Olivier so he could *be* him.

It was Capitaine Philippe Brevard who had tracked St Priest down, who had brought me out of the dark abyss of grief. Who I had married months later, on the courthouse steps in Metz.

Perhaps it was a flash of the bad memories that haunt me. Being trapped in the back of a car filled with explosives. Wrestling for the gun. If I looked hard, he would go away.

He did not go away. He did not seem to see me. To be aware that I had stopped suddenly six feet from the chairs and tables in front of the cafe, to be aware that he held a cold, sick grip on me, dead though he was. I stumbled, and a man in a hurry bumped into me.

'Désolé.'

'Pardon.'

The man gave me a quick nod and walked away.

Charl St Priest was still there, looking past me with that haughty, smug smile that I would dread for the rest of my life. I turned to see who he was smiling at, and the air went out of my lungs.

Béatrice. God. And she *did* meet my eyes, like she was waiting for me to catch sight of her. She looked exactly as she had the last time I had seen her. The same air of malevolence beneath the innocent facade. She was tall. Thick dark hair cut just at her collarbone, her dark eyes intense. The top of her head was blown off. She had already been dead when I shot her, just for good measure, her slender delicate neck broken, eyes wide. I felt the heat in my cheeks and took her smile for a threat.

And then she turned away, as if St Priest was all that kept her there. She gave him that look of intimate frisson that I knew too well, and it was as if something physical passed between the two of them, the danger they emanated forming like crystals in the air, and then she passed right through me and I felt an agonizing shock that tingled from one nerve ending to the next.

I settled carefully at the closest table, gripping the arms of the metal chair. The cafe had just opened, and the owner nodded at me. I was a regular, he knew my order and would bring it soon. I studied the street. Early fog and chill, my hair heavy with humidity. I took a long breath in and out, before I was compelled to look back over my shoulder.

They were gone. Béatrice and St Priest.

And I knew it as a warning. An omen. Blood and carnage.

My three minutes were up.

I didn't have long to wait.

TWO

I saw my death in the tall, well-muscled man striding toward me. How he looked at me in a way that was full of anguish and appeal . . . and strangely holy. I knew he brought danger; I saw the fear in his eyes. And I understood that my life was never going to be the same.

I had not heard his approach, but my hearing dog, Leo, a glorious one-hundred-pound German Shepherd, gave me a nudge and I looked up from my cold cup of coffee.

I knew this man. I knew his wife even better.

Stéphane Morel owned a small dairy farm with a newly built home on a modest acreage of family land near the Glières Plateau. Morel had a small but prize-winning herd of Abondance cattle, which he milked by hand twice daily, to make the Abondance cheese that had earned the AOC quality mark – Appellation d'origine controlée – since 1990.

His little farm was a tiny bit of paradise, and he worked long hours to make it that way, but the peace would soon be destroyed by billionaire 'Daddy' Sullivan Carr's plans to build a bitcoin mine nearby, dangerously close to one of the best places in the world for cross-country skiing, where they currently hold Nordic Nights every Thursday, and you can ski under a star-filled sky.

Turning beauty into hell zones. A specialty of the very rich.

An outrageous plan, even for a dick-swinging billionaire.

Within the last two weeks the rumors had begun. Daddy Sullivan Carr had come to the attention of the dark and lethal secret society of Les Vipères Emeraudes – The Emerald Vipers.

Within the hour it will be more than just a rumor.

I was afraid of The Emerald Vipers. You should be too.

THREE

I was aware that people were staring at Stéphane, the palpable danger in his walk. It had been some time since the city of Annecy had been stunned and violated by a mentally ill knife-wielding attacker who had gone after small children in Le Pâquier park. They were watchful now; wary.

Stéphane stopped in front of my table, and the look he gave me was haunted. Leo was already up on his feet. Utterly silent. Head low.

'What is it, Stéphane?'

He handed me a large envelope. The flap was torn open.

'Sit,' I told him.

He frowned at me, as if he struggled to understand the word, then pulled out a chair and sat. His long, strong legs did not fit under the table. Leo stayed on his feet, leaning hard against my leg.

It was a plain brown envelope, eight by eleven inches, smudged with dirt, with my name, address, phone number, office address, email address, age and physical description and favorite coffee shops printed in a very long list at the top.

I got the point.

'It's addressed to me. How did you get this?'

His voice was flat and hard. 'It was hand delivered to me this morning.'

He ran large square hands over his face. In his late thirties, he had dark eyes, longish chestnut hair. His face was lined by long hours of physical labor and sun. A farmer's face.

He stared over my shoulder, his voice robotic. Shock.

He had been out in the barn, had just finished milking the cows, and a woman had sauntered in with a smug face and an air of amusement at being in an actual *barn*. She admitted she was not rural. She had never seen a cow up close. She was shocked to find that cows were surprisingly *large*.

Then she got down to business, introducing herself with matter-of-fact honesty and no actual name. She was part of a for-hire military security team, kitted up in an armored vest, lethal weapon on her hip. She asked him ever so nicely to personally deliver the envelope to Junie Lagarde. When he demanded to know what it was all about, she asked if he had talked to his wife since she left for work, laughed, and headed out the wide-open entrance of the barn.

Stéphane's wife was my lead journalist, Analise Morel. She was also seven months pregnant.

I had taken the climate change NGO I had inherited upon the death of Olivier and used it to fund VIE. Vérité, Information, Égalité – Truth, Information, Equality. VIE's open-source investigative journalism was an out-and-out takedown of billionaires who made money on climate change atrocities. Who thought they could plunder the world and take with impunity.

Analise had a madly successful podcast called *Billionaires Behaving Badly* that was posted on the VIE website twice a week. VIE held billionaires accountable. We knew who to blame.

We also pissed them off.

Stéphane's voice was wooden. 'I called her, my wife, over and over. I called the office. Nobody answered.'

'You called the landline at VIE?' There should have been three or four people at the office now, including Analise. Most of my staff did not get up early in the morning so much as not sleep during the night.

Stéphane nodded. When he could not get Analise on the phone, he had opened the envelope, but the paper inside made no sense to him. He knew it was bad, but he didn't get how. He'd tried to call me, but he said my phone was on Do Not Disturb. Which it was. I made a quick check. Other than three calls from my husband, Philippe, who I was ignoring at the moment, Stéphane had called me six times.

I hit the number on my phone for VIE.

'Anything?' Stéphane asked.

'Disconnected.'

Stéphane leaned close, taking up the space of the small table, watching me dump the contents of the envelope.

An old poster from *Three Days of the Condor*. Robert Redford and Faye Dunaway locked in an embrace, surrounded by shadowy, dangerous men. A movie where a CIA analyst who spent his time gathering information, went out to lunch and returned to find all of his colleagues dead. All of them gathering information the old-school way. Gathering information like VIE did the new-school way.

Down at the bottom, in a dark scrawl of black ink: *Condolences from Sullivan Carr.* Our current billionaire in the crosshairs.

'What is this?' Stéphane asked.

'Putain de mauvaise nouvelle,' I told him. Fucking bad news. Because I knew exactly what it was. 'It's a threat. They're at the office. They're at VIE.'

And instantly I was up out of my chair and on the run, with Leo beside me, and Stéphane overtaking me with long strides.

FOUR

The office of VIE was located in an apartment on Rue Jean-Jacques Rousseau, which was two streets away, in the heart of the city, near the Square de l'Evêché.

Outside on the pavement, broken glass from shattered French doors glinted in the sunlight. People were looking up at the office. I heard sirens in the distance. The police station across the street, hemmed in now by pedestrian streets, was dark and deserted as it usually was. The real law enforcement business was on the other side of town.

Fuck.

I thundered up the twisting concrete stairs, Leo by my side, with Stéphane Morel now two steps ahead of me. I heard shots. Two of them.

The door to the apartment was ajar, and Leo began to bark.

It was a total shitshow.

FIVE

There was blood pooling and streaming into the hallway. The sharp acrid scent of gunpowder. The first two bodies were in the bright living room that looked out over Quai de l'Evêché, with the fireplace that did not work.

Blood trails. My staff. Staring at me with glassy eyes, because they were gone. Just gone.

Louis Romilly, Research. Clementine Allard, Visual Analysis.

I could see the legs of another body in the kitchen. Heavy motorcycle boots. Timothée Fornier, Master of Tech, a job title he came up with himself. Just last week he had set up two digital counters at the bottom of the website. One kept track of billionaires by name and the number of people who have died as a direct result of their investment in the destruction of the earth. We called that one ECOCIDE. The other one, GO FOR IT, BABE, kept track of every single action we could gather up that countered climate change atrocities. That one got the most submissions. Click for details.

Blood flowed copiously out from under Timothée's head in rivulets that snaked and flowed and pooled on the kitchen floor.

High-power weapons shred a body in ways that are shocking to see up close. Our freshly painted walls were splashed with brain matter, bits of bone, and blood. A lot of blood. Our BILLIONAIRES SUCK banner hung sideways, but it was still up on the wall.

A man and a woman were waiting for us. Dressed in black, heavily armed, encased in armored vests. Were they afraid we'd throw a computer at them?

'Ah, there you are, Monsieur Morel. Your wife has locked herself in the bathroom, holding her belly. I hope we have not sent her into early labor.'

Leo's head was low and he was ready to leap. I put a hand on his collar, felt how he was quivering, heard the deep-chested growl.

The woman gave Morel a sympathetic look. 'My associate here will take you to your wife.' She tilted her head sideways. 'I do not like this dog who looks at me like a wolf who does not understand the power of the bullet.'

'If you want to get to my dog you'll have to go through me.'
She was unimpressed. 'That is actually the point.'

If I had had the large and lethal handgun she was pointing down at the ground, I would have shot her in the face. If I had had the large and lethal handgun she was pointing down at the ground, I would have emptied the cartridge into her body without regret.

When I had pissed off a powerful billionaire, I had been worried about lawsuits, not a death squad. You might say that I'd been very good at my job.

Maybe I should have seen this coming. Billionaires were known to have epic tantrums when things did not go their way. And no one sends out a death squad unless they are threatened and afraid.

And to make a point. To make sure no one crosses them ever again. Carr was one of the wealthy elite, basking in the glow of knowing he could get away with anything, anytime, anywhere.

The man motioned to Stéphane. 'I will take you to your wife. You would like to see her, I think.'

Stéphane looked at me over his shoulder, and I saw it in his face. He would go down fighting, but we were all of us dead.

Leo whimpered and strained forward. I was starting to wonder if I could hold him back. To wonder if I should.

The woman held the gun up, took aim. 'It is a split second to shoot you in the face.'

'Would you like a cup of coffee?' I asked. 'I'll make some for all of us, and you can drink yours after I'm dead.'

The woman gave me a puzzled look. 'Stay where you are. I want you to hear what is happening next.'

I didn't want to hear it. Sometimes it's good to have a hearing loss. But I caught bits. Murmurs from Stéphane. Then the man's voice, quite loud. 'Recording the death of Analise Morel.'

A door slammed open. Then one shot, a body hitting the floor.

The woman smiled broadly. Held up her phone, centering my face on the camera. 'I have a message for you from Sullivan Carr.'

'And I have one for him. Fuck all y'all.'

She adjusted the phone one inch higher. 'Recording the death of Junie Lagarde.'

'Hang on, I'm going in the kitchen to make that coffee.' It took a split second to get out of camera range and drag Leo into the kitchen. A hopeless last-ditch effort to get my dog out of the line of fire. Timothée was on his side, face to the floor, eyes open, unseeing. The cutlery drawer was partly open and I realized he had a knife still clutched in his fist. The paring knife so useful for cutting cheese, fruit, and possibly assassins. For a split second I thought his hand twitched. Leo went to sniff him and I tried to put him in a down stay. He overruled me which is why more Golden Retrievers become service dogs than German Shepherds. I grabbed his collar and he lost his shit, whimpering and barking and twisting from side to side, and it could be the only thing Sullivan Carr was going to see on his video was me in a wrestling match with my dog. Leo was in the red zone now and I wasn't going to be able to hold him.

The woman followed us in. Held up her phone to get a good angle. The red dot sight lines of a sniper rifle played across the top of her head.

'Recording the death of Junie Lagarde,' she repeated.

I threw myself over Leo, sliding in Timothée's blood. The woman hit the ground before I did, dead before she dropped. Leo and I went down hard, my left ankle twisting in an excruciating inward rotation.

Leo scrambled back up on his feet in a split second. Me not so much. Looking at the angle of my ankle made me sick to my stomach. So did the pain.

Leo positioned himself over me and began to emit high, sharp, staccato barks. The official position and call for help of the German Shepherd.

I heard more sirens in the distance. Footsteps in the street, shouts, and someone thundering toward the kitchen. Male. Heavy. Fast.

I did not know what to do. Not make coffee was all I could think of.

SIX

He came into the room at a brisk pace, took a look around, a sleek and lethal sniper rifle over one shoulder. He was about five foot eight, stocky with the thick muscular physique of a professional wrestler, collar-length dark blond hair. Lines in his face. He had the look of a man who'd led a hard life. A lot of it out in the sun.

'Bonjour, madame.'

'There's another one in the back, they just killed—'

'No, no, madame, he is dead.'

'He – *Leo. Silence.*' And it came to me. I had only heard one shot. 'You killed the other guy?'

'Of course, that is why I am here. And the beautiful pregnant lady and her husband are OK. I got them out the back door.'

'There isn't a back door.'

'I made one.' He took a quick glance at the woman on the floor. 'Merde, I *cannot* believe this. My aim was off; it should have been a head shot, not the throat, though of course, that works very well.' He looked at Leo and slapped his chest. 'Hush now, you beautiful boy, and come here to me.'

Leo lunged toward him and did what I call the leap of affection, giving the man a kiss full square on the lips. He grinned at me over Leo's shoulder, ruffling his fur. 'I am a Shepherd guy, he knows this.'

I had seen this before. Leo walking nicely, then suddenly taking a shine to some big guy who greeted him like a long-lost love. *Shepherd guys.*

He gave me a half smile. 'Why are you on the floor? I know very well I did not shoot you.' He pointed to the couch. 'Go sit down there, you are getting your jacket drenched in blood, that is going to stain the leather.'

'I have twisted my ankle so I actually can't.'

The man crossed the room to peer down at me. Leo got there first, sniffing my neck.

'I am Guiorgui Cambronne. Though mostly I am called La Puce.'

'The flea?'

'Yes. In the US they would call me The Hulk or The Brute, but in France we must make the joke.'

'But who are you officially? Isn't there a SWAT team or something?'

He grinned. 'The hostage team assembles as we speak. They got here very fast; the police here are quite good. They worry about hostages, and are organizing, and will move in about four minutes and before that I must leave. Me, I am a . . . negotiator.'

'And you negotiate by—'

'Killing them? Yes. It is the best way to negotiate. We cannot let them live.'

He pulled a small envelope out of his jacket pocket. Gave a little bow and looked down at me. 'Please, take this envelope and know that you are under the protection of Les Vipères Emeraudes.'

'The Emerald Vipers,' I said softly, tucking the envelope inside my shirt.

'I work for them, yes. You know of us?'

'How could I not? Whoever's in charge of your dark PR does a hell of a job.'

'You will hear more.' He gave me a serious look. 'Inside that envelope you will find a letter of apology. Please keep this private and do not share with the gendarmerie.'

'An apology for what?'

'It has not gone unnoticed, your work and what you do. We cheer you on, as you Americans say. We have the same goal, to take down the billionaire class. Also the apology is for what we do next. Also we do not wish to upset your husband. He has a reputation in the law-enforcement community.'

'Philippe? He's a sweetheart.'

'To you I am sure, madame.' He sighed. 'It is good we got some of you safe, but this never should have happened. We feel very bad. Sadly, this attack is our fault. We sent Sullivan Carr the emerald of death already and yet it is you he blames. Really we do not get the credit we deserve, though I say that your website is helpful, and embedded with metadata so everything can be proven and verified. We admire your operation very much. We will be watching over you now; we won't let this happen again.'

'Again?'

'We may even ask for your help. You are crucial; we will all work together.'

'I don't work with terrorists.'

He smiled. 'I am confident that I can change your mind. You will be receiving an invitation soon. Do please attend our ceremony on Pont des Amours at the end of the week.'

'What kind of ceremony are you having on the bridge of love? Does this have something to do with the emerald of death that you sent Sullivan Carr?'

'Exactement. That we will do this during Le Carnaval Vénitien is an inspiration of genius, I think. It is theatre, and it will impress. It will happen at the stroke of midnight. Go early, we expect a crowd.' He paused. 'If Sullivan Carr is angry now, you must expect him to lose his mind by the end of the week.'

Leo huffed. He looked at me, then back to the hallway, letting me know someone was there. La Puce looked up sharply. Leo huffed again and I had that flash of vulnerability I feel when my hearing loss means I am unaware of things happening all around me. A world without Leo was a world where I would never be safe.

'Footsteps,' La Puce said. 'There is a man in the hallway walking toward us.'

He talked like a man who knew about my hearing loss, and that worried me. Too many people knew things about me. 'I thought you said you got Analise and her husband out.'

'Oui, both of them are out and safe. But someone has come in.' There was now a gun in his hand, the rifle still over his shoulder.

'Maybe he got in through the new back door.'

He frowned, then tilted his head to one side and put the gun away, beckoning the man into the room, a big smile on his face. 'Look who has joined us. It is Le Sorcier. I introduce you, Madame Lagarde, to The Wizard. We call him that because you never see him coming.'

I gave the man a wary look. 'He is one of Les Vipères Emeraudes?'

Le Sorcier studied me with an intensity that was almost mesmerizing. 'Bonjour, Madame Lagarde. And I am most certainly *not* one of Les Vipères. These days Cambronne and I find ourselves on opposite sides. But many years ago . . .' He shrugged.

La Puce nodded. 'Many years ago, we fought together in La Légion étrangère. The French foreign legion. Now he works for billionaires.'

'You work for Sullivan Carr?'

Le Sorcier shrugged. 'As you see . . . je suis en retard à la fête.'

'Late to the party?' I said very hard. Looking at the bodies of my staff. At the blood.

'Désolé, madame. I did not mean to offend.' His glanced over at me, his eyes intensely blue.

He wore blue jeans, a black sweater and a black leather jacket, ankle-high hiking boots. My boots were leather with flashy buckles and not as practical as his, otherwise we were dressed almost exactly the same. His hair was light brown with a lot of gray, cheeks rough with a two-day growth of grey-flecked beard.

He gave La Puce a half smile. They clasped arms just below the elbow.

'You are more than late,' La Puce said. 'Everyone is dead or rescued except this one, Madame Lagarde, who is under my protection.' He turned to me with a smile. 'You must not worry about Le Sorcier when he has the full head of hair.'

If that was a joke it went over my head.

Le Sorcier shrugged. 'You see, mon pote, my buddy, I initially turned this job down. I did not like the terms or the pay. I do not kill pregnant women or dogs, and I charge triple what they offered. But I have been called in at the last minute as things clearly did not go so well.' He shook his head. 'Half-assed military for hire branching out as cut-rate assassins. Vous en avez pour votre argent.'

You get what you pay for.

Le Sorcier put a hand to his chin, and walked slowly around the room, taking everything in, stopping for a moment to bend close to the still-warm body of the woman La Puce had killed. 'Bad shot on this one.'

Leo moved toward him, but La Puce grabbed him by the collar, and I scrambled to get up and failed.

'Leo, with me.'

Le Sorcier had a voice that was kind and oddly soothing. 'Little doggie, your mama is OK, and I will not hurt her. *For now.*'

La Puce narrowed his eyes. Watched as Le Sorcier bent over to look at me.

'You are not shot?'

'I slipped and fell.'

'Quoi?'

'In the blood, I slipped.'

'Ah yes, it is like black ice on pavement.' He shook his head, looking grim. 'It looks at a bad angle to me, your ankle. We will get you up.'

He nodded at La Puce and with one assassin on either side, they lifted me up and sat me on the couch, ignoring my small screams of pain. Just sitting was a relief, but my ankle was sideways, and when Le Sorcier reached toward my foot, I grabbed his hand.

'*Don't*. Don't touch it.'

'As you wish. You must have this seen at the ankle clinic. I am sorry to say you are going to need surgery. With the doctors on strike, I just hope they can get you in, but they should be staffed if you go in through emergency.'

La Puce cocked his head to one side. 'More sirens. We have ninety seconds. You will leave first, Le Sorcier.'

Le Sorcier nodded. 'Be aware, both of you, that there are two other teams in town. It is like a convention here, with as many assassins as tourists.'

'Two?' La Puce frowned. 'Surely not. I have only clocked one, not counting these idiots.'

'Two,' Le Sorcier repeated. 'But to be sure, none of them very good.'

I felt a tiny bit disrespected. 'Why is Sullivan Carr hiring bad assassins if he has all the money in the world?'

La Puce made a rude noise. 'The good ones will not work for guys like Carr. Governments pay more and to deal with them is not such a pain in the ass. So, I am telling *you* now, mon pote, as you have only just been hired, you might want to tell Sullivan Carr you changed your mind. Because I will kill you if you try to finish this job.'

Le Sorcier gave me a smile. 'You are safe for now, madame. I am here merely to observe and report back. Au revoir, madame. Au revoir le petit chien. I am sorry to leave you this way, when you are hurt like this.' He turned away and disappeared toward the back of the apartment.

La Puce waited, listening to things I could not hear. The sound of Le Sorcier leaving perhaps . . . maybe the police below in the street. Even with Leo, I missed a lot of what was going on.

He gave me a kind smile. 'I also must go, but you will be in good hands now. Bon courage, madame.'

Leo, who knew his job, stood beside me and began another series of short staccato barks. He was calling for help again. Evidently, he had no confidence in hitmen.

SEVEN

The Deputy Commander of the Annecy Gendarmerie, Capitaine Dauphine Babineaux, was a hard ass and she and I were not getting along. She wore the uniform blue jacket with epaulets over a blue polo shirt and sat across from me speaking in a calm voice that was relentless and so rapid fire that I missed as much as I heard.

Emergency services had wrapped me in a gold foil blanket, which was warm but not cuddly. They had given me water, which I had shared with Leo, and eased my left foot into a protective boot. After they had swiped my hands for gunshot residue, I was allowed to clean most of the blood off my hands and face. Police officers were trampling up and down the stairs, the media was heavy on the sidewalk, and the street outside had been barricaded. Sirens came and went.

Capitaine Babineaux did not believe my story, and she had good reason not to. Analise and Stéphane were missing.

Where was the envelope with the movie poster? And Sullivan Carr would not sign his name to such a thing, it was ridiculous.

Why did I not first call the police if I thought there was a threat to my staff?

Why would an important man like Sullivan Carr care about my little website in France?

If this was a death squad hit on VIE, why was I, the owner of VIE, not the first one dead?

What was open-source intelligence? She had never heard of this; people do not send assassins to deal with websites.

In my favor . . .

Yes, the body of the assassin who had led Stéphane down the hall was lying half in and out of the bathroom, one shot to the head. Yes, the body of the assassin who had been recording my death had been shot through the throat right outside the kitchen. Yes, a six-by-three-foot opening had been cut between our office and the apartment behind us that was used as an Airbnb, currently unoccupied. Yes, the front door of that apartment was unlocked.

Yes, the briefcase of Analise Morel had been found in the bathroom with her laptop.

The search for weapons turned up nothing but the knife in Timothée's fist, but empty cartridges were thick on the ground.

My insistence that there was not one, not two but a total of four assassins, not all of them on the same side, but all gathered in the carnage of my office, did not go over well. Babineaux made a hissing noise that Leo did not like.

'Une farce absolue,' she said.

I explained yet again that VIE was an organization of open-source intelligence investigative journalists. That billionaires buy up media to push their agendas and influence and that journalists are under attack all over the world, particularly women. Nine times out of ten, the murder of a journalist is unresolved.

'Don't take my word for it, look at the latest UNESCO report.'

That got her attention.

'I assure you, Madame Lagarde, that this *will* be resolved. If you are truly being targeted by Sullivan Carr, we will not hesitate to pursue this.'

'What more do you need? He signed the threat.'

'I have one of my officers looking for the poster, which I have yet to see, and is conveniently lost. But it is ridiculous to believe that the one who set this up would have signed his name. It feels like he is being set up. By you, perhaps?'

'The ridiculous person here is you. They were *recording* our deaths.'

'So you say, but we have yet to find a phone from either of the assassins. Someone who would do a job like this would not bring a phone or anything to identify them.'

'They would if the one who hired them wanted to see it unfold in real life.'

She shrugged. 'I do not think you or VIE are important enough for such a man to hate.'

'Then you don't understand the mindset of someone who is never told no; who thinks they are above the law, which get real, they are—'

'They are not above the law in France.'

'I wish I believed that.'

'How can something like this VIE make enough trouble for a man like this? Other than his ego, and the ego of men like this is well known, but *assassins*?'

'We are costing him money.' I explained about the bitcoin mine that Carr was planning to build. That got a frown. She'd heard of that. She didn't know what such a thing was and why it mattered. So I told her the reality of a bitcoin mine and why it did matter. That bitcoin mines were filled with cooling fans and computers that solved complex math equations to verify transactions in cryptocurrency. That they had all the environmental impact of a coal-burning plant with none of the charm. That if this mine was built, she could expect her energy bills to double and then triple over the next three years.'

She gave me a look of shock.

'And since we've been covering this, a lot of people in Annecy are fighting it. We do in-depth articles. Analise Morel has a twice-weekly podcast called *Billionaires Behaving Badly*.'

'And you put Carr on this broadcast?'

'Yes. We've been going after him hard. Eighty percent of his portfolio is emissions intensive. The average billionaire produces more emissions in three hours than the average person does in a lifetime. It only takes Carr *one* hour. So we report it, along with all the other stuff he spends money on. Twelve million dollars for a shark preserved in formaldehyde which he calls art, two million for a picture of Billy the Kid—'

'The outlaw of the American West?'

I took a moment. Gritted my teeth. 'Yes, the outlaw of the American West.'

'That is ridiculous to pay such money.'

'It's nothing to him. He has a twenty-million-dollar car collection, and he has cars flown to wherever he travels. He sends them ahead, also on a jet, so they are ready for him when he gets off his plane. He has his own island, and a sixteen-million-dollar Badminton Cabinet at his horse farm in Kentucky.'

She was frowning. It was the two million for Billy the Kid that had hit home. 'Why does he care really that you tell people about this? A man like that wants people to know; he will brag about it.'

'Wrong. Billionaires *don't* want people to know. Carr wants his privacy. And he does *not* want to be ridiculed.'

'And you ridicule him?'

'We report what he is doing, so he ridicules himself. And . . . since we have been going after his bitcoin mine, he is being harassed by . . .' I trailed off. I couldn't say it.

'Harassed by what?'

'Bigfoot.'

She shut her eyes very tight.

The officer taking notes nodded. 'But this is true, Capitaine, I have heard of this, and we have had to go out and investigate complaints from the sight where he is building the mine.'

'He is actually building it?' she asked.

'Oui, Capitaine, as she says, on the plateau, I take my girlfriend there to ski. It is very romantic.'

She glared at him, then looked at me. 'Explain this.'

It had started with a baker's blog, from one of the restaurants in Cran-Gevrier. An ad campaign where they had pictures of Bigfoot on a walking trail eating one of their baguettes. Somehow it had taken hold and evolved into a protest movement where Bigfoot would ski at Carr's construction sight, eating a baguette. Bigfoot hanging from a crane, eating a baguette. Bigfoot sitting at a picnic table with construction workers, eating a baguette. There was graffiti, and vandalism. BIGFOOT ETAIT LA. Bigfoot was here.

And the mine construction that had been going forward at a worrisome clip was starting to hit snags.

'Sullivan Carr does not like snags,' I told her.

She was thinking hard, listening, but I could not read her at all.

'And now he's hit more than a snag,' I said. 'Les Vipères Emeraudes.'

'The Vipères who you tell me saved your life, introduced themselves to you, and gave you their card.'

'You have it in an evidence bag.'

'I tell you this, Madame Lagarde. We know this group. A dark and lethal secret society, and if you are working with them—'

'Half my staff just got gunned down, Capitaine Babineaux. I am not working with anybody but VIE.'

The officer held out his phone. 'This is the VIE website, Capitaine.'

She took the phone, scrolled through. Looked up at me. 'You have made Carr a joke on *The Daily Show*?'

'They picked it up, yes.'

'Memes,' she said. 'Your last broadcast had two and a half million hits?'

'And rising. And the journalist behind the podcasts is Analise Morel.'

'And the other assassin, number four, who wanders through for no particular reason. How do you explain that?'

'You think I know? But I think he's working for Carr.'

'And for what reason would he be there afterward, if not to kill you? If he—' She stopped. Frowning.

'The phones. He came to get the phones the assassins used to record our deaths live, for Sullivan Carr. Which are proof.'

'Only if we find them; they will be burner phones.' She took a breath and let it out slowly. 'And you say this is Carr's revenge?'

'He doesn't just want revenge.'

'What then?' she asked.

'Everything.'

EIGHT

When my husband arrived, I was in a state of hysteria and a heated argument with Capitaine Babineaux.

I looked up just as Philippe walked into the room, careful of glass and blood, and Capitaine Babineaux glared up in wide-open fury, inclining her head to one of the officers.

I was so happy to see Philippe that I sobbed.

'Get him *out*,' Capitaine Babineaux said.

'I am her husband. I will stay.'

Grim of mouth, dark haired, hazel eyes. A steadiness that always made me feel safe in the world. He'd driven in from Metz, and his tie was loose, shirt collar unbuttoned. Charcoal-grey suit, leather shoes with tassels – he'd been in court today with the judge he worked for, doing private investigations since he'd been fired as a capitaine of the police over a year ago. He'd been in charge of the investigation into the death of my husband, Olivier, who had gone down in a plane over Mont Blanc. It was Philippe who had given me the news of my Olivier's death, who had taken me to view the body, Olivier still handsome though great swathes of his flesh had been charred from the fire and the carnage after his small plane crashed on the bleak and deadly plateau. Leo had pulled Olivier and the pilot out of the plane, and my husband had died with Leo by his side. It was Philippe who discovered the plane had been sabotaged.

There are those who were enraged by the way Philippe was treated when he stopped a terrorist attack on the Mont Blanc Tunnel. He chose the lives of his officers over millions of euros of damage to the tunnel, and was offered the faux face-saving opportunity to resign. Philippe had refused and had been fired. The judge took great pleasure in working with Philippe, and I think he was hired to score political points and piss people off as much as he was hired for his rather formidable intellect and skill set. The wealthy elite in France have circles and layers of grudges and one-upmanship that interest me not at all.

But one thing was clear. The more power people have in the world, the more they loathe a man like Philippe, who prefers human life over the inconvenience of expense. Very much like my first husband, Olivier, who died for it.

'Ah, Philippe, it is you,' Capitaine Babineaux said now. 'It's been a while since we met. I must ask you to step away for a bit, you understand that—'

He ignored her. Sat down beside me on the couch and held my hand. 'I am here,' he said in a low voice. It was all I needed to hear. He reached out to pet Leo, murmuring softly. 'Tu va bien, mon fiston.' You're OK, old son.

Leo was stretched out on the floor beside my feet, breathing hard. A young gendarme had brought him a bowl of water an hour ago and he'd lapped all of it up. My anxiety had become his anxiety; we were always in sync.

'How long have you been interrogating my wife, Dauphine?' Philippe's voice was hard.

'We are in an emergency here, Philippe, and Madame Lagarde's story is not adding up.'

'My wife has a hearing loss, perhaps she made you aware of that? No? It is quite an effort for her to understand what you say with all of this noise, and the experience she has been through, can you not see how exhausted she is? She is in pain, most likely in shock, and I am taking her now to the Clinique Générale. You can meet with us there if you must.'

She pursed her lips. Thinking. Unhappy with both of us.

'My story isn't going to change,' I told her.

An officer thundered up the stairs and went to her side where they had a quick, low-toned discussion. He handed her an evidence bag with the brown envelope and movie poster. I had left it on the table in the coffee shop. The owner had gathered it up for me. I drank coffee there every day, and he had seen an agitated and panicked Stéphane Morel approach me that morning with the envelope in hand.

Capitaine Babineaux let us go. For now.

NINE

'Philippe, please, just take me home.'
'No, madame, you must be seen, I think that ankle is broken.'
'Please.'
'This is France, Junie. Things are different here. Everything will be OK.'

Philippe knew me well. I could not go to a doctor or a hospital without that sick feeling most Americans get. I preferred death to medical care, unless I was in pain. It was always the pain that got you through the door.

No matter how much I knew, logically and with many assurances from Philippe, that things were different in France, my fear of the snarls and layers of financial disaster caused by walking into an ER in the US had given me an ingrained horror of medical bills. When I was an accountant for elder care clients, I had come away with a deep-rooted horror of the system.

It was a short drive to the clinic, and Philippe did not ask me any questions about what happened, just told me I would be OK. As if I could ever be OK again. I put my head on his shoulder.

'They're gone,' I said. 'Forever gone. Clementine, Louis, Timothée. How can that be? And Stéphane and Analise. That man, the one who killed the assassins. He said they were safe, that they got away. But Capitaine Babineaux said they were nowhere to be found, and that was why she was grilling me so hard. Where are they? Are they even still alive? I need to see them. I need to make sure they're all right.'

Philippe frowned. 'What is this word? Grill?'

I sighed.

'Junie, there is a lot of confusion, with something like this. They are likely OK, but yes, I am worried too. Once I get you settled, I will call Babineaux and ask.'

'She won't tell you anything.'

'She will.'

He took my hand and held it, driving easily, letting me talk it out.

They were young; my whole staff was so *young*. Babies. I wondered if they would blame me. Their families. If I were them, I would blame me. I would blame me all to hell. And me, I had slipped in their blood. I had fallen. How stupid was that when they were laying dead on the floor? Turned the ankle in an excruciatingly unnatural torque, and the first thing the doctors would tell me was that it would never heal back properly. That's what they always said in the US, and then they handed you a preprinted sheet with two exercises, as if that was close to what you needed to do for rehab. And also, the little illustrations were always wrong, which for some reason was the norm. But I had hurt my ankle before; I *knew* what to do, because if you did not come up with a healing regimen and stick with it for a year, you would not heal. You had to put in the time.

And I knew this because I had healed plenty of injuries years ago, back when I was riding horses, because you cannot ride horses without getting hurt, not me anyway, and I had owned a beautiful mare who had died two years ago, had I told him that?

'I don't think you have. I did not know you had a horse.'

'She was beautiful, but spooky, full of fears and triggers and hot to hand.' I told him how the mare had dumped me on my ass more than once, and then stood over me in the field, nuzzling the top of my head in apology, and I had whispered to her over and over: *It's OK. My fault. I forget sometimes how afraid you are.*

But that was the thing about horses. Their lives were a crapshoot of loving owners, brutal owners, or negligent ones. And they arrived in your life, veterans of a world of experience you had no idea about. A lot of it not good. Not good at all.

'I miss her, Philippe. I loved her so much.'

Philippe did not seem at all puzzled about how the conversation had turned to horses, and he held my hand very tight.

I didn't realize I had fallen asleep until Philippe woke me.

'Stay here for a moment, madame, with Leo. I will be right back.'

Minutes later Philippe had settled me into a wheelchair and was guiding me through the door for Accès Urgences. Annecy was a good place for sports medicine and the center was staffed with surgeons, sports doctors of the locomotor system, even a sports psychologist. The doctors were on strike and had been for three days, but emergency services were available. Just as Le Sorcier had said.

The x-rays showed an old, calcified bone fragment from an injury I didn't remember, and the bones intact. A rupture of the Achilles tendon was at first suspected, and would require surgery, and a minimum one year to heal, but then it was decided, God knows how, that I had a fibular tendon dislocation, which sounded to me like a sprained ankle, which was painful, but would not require surgery after all.

We had spent three hours in the center, long enough in waiting rooms for me to tell Philippe everything.

I did not understand what had happened, I told him with my voice going tight. My story of assassins coming and going had been met by Capitaine Dauphine with a hard-faced disbelief, but there were two bodies of military assassins to back me up and no gunpowder residue on my hands.

Philippe was thinking hard, and he squeezed my hand, face set in lines of a calm, lethal rage. He had not taken it well, this attack on VIE, and my story of La Puce and Le Sorcier resulted in a red flush of fury, even though La Puce had saved my life.

Leo was tucked by the plastic chairs where we waited for them to schedule my initial appointment of physical therapy and rehabilitation, head between paws, looking lethargic, looking depressed, and he sat up and whimpered, only settling when Philippe stroked his head and called him 'mon fiston' again.

'I know this man, Junie. This La Puce.'

'He seems to know you.'

'I need to step outside and make a few calls. You will be OK, here with Leo?'

I nodded, and he kissed me. I wondered who he was calling. And why he hadn't told me who.

He was gone for long time, and was just coming back in when I was being released with paperwork and detailed instructions that I was too tired to make any sense of. There must be a determination of an Ankle-GO score before I could return to sport. I had been approved for physiotherapy by the specialist but could not yet be scheduled for my first appointment, as there could be delays due to the strike.

It did not worry me.

I would go to the pharmacist down the road if I needed anything – and mainly what I wanted was Advil. I knew the prescribed pain pills would make me sick. The two they had given me in the emergency room were making me miserable already, but they were also putting me to sleep. I had been tossed off a few horses in my life. I knew how to rehab an ankle.

TEN

There is fallout when people are gunned down at your feet. Clean-up. Bloodstains. Exhaustion.

Philippe had kept me on my feet while I showered. I was too wobbly to stand on my own, and I was just beginning to understand how this ankle injury was going to trash my balance. He'd given me one of his old soft sweaters to wear, then settled me on the couch with my ankle elevated and iced. He had fed Leo, who would not eat, then given him a good scrubbing until he too was soft and clean and smelled like lavender shampoo.

Leo was asleep now, sound asleep. His chest rose and fell as he snored softly beside me on the couch, head resting on my stomach, and I was pinned down but happy to have him close. He looked adorable with a new green plaid bow tie on his new leather collar. The old ones had been encrusted in blood, and Philippe had thrown them away, a first step at easing the trauma from our lives.

It had been a long, unbearable day.

Philippe told me he was going out to pick up some food that I knew I would not be able to eat. There were lines of exhaustion etched into his face, and he looked grim and determined, *not* like a man going out for food. I heard his footsteps as he went down the stairs, a man in a hurry. I wondered about the calls he had made.

I tried to sleep, but when I closed my eyes I would see it, an imprint on my brain. Timothée in the kitchen, flannel shirt soaked with blood, so much blood, pools and pools of it, clutching the kitchen knife, eyes open. Sometimes in my memory his fingers moved.

There were too many thoughts in my head. Would I ever be able to walk into that office again? Should I move VIE to another location? Should I let the rest of the staff go with a generous severance package just for their own safety? Anyone could find us wherever we were.

Why had I not seen this coming? How had I still not wrapped my mind around the realization that the world was a billionaire's boardroom? American corporations had been sending out death squads for decades – Chiquita was one of the first to be held responsible. Corporate whistleblowers for Boeing had a strange habit of committing suicide.

But even a billionaire like Sullivan Carr would be no match for the information that came to VIE day in and day out from average people all over the world. Citizen journalists. There were too many of us. I would not give up on VIE. My little website had not impressed Capitaine Babineaux, but it had made a billionaire afraid.

Sleep was strangely impossible; I could not be still. I went softly out to the balcony, grabbed the railing and lowered myself slowly, sitting on the old linoleum surface, hidden away in the dark. It had been raining softly for the last hour, and now had stopped. It seemed to rain all the time here. In Kentucky I had grown used to the murderous heat, the ice storms, and the tornados. Annecy weather was a gentle thing.

I thought again of my staff . . . so young. So full of energy, busy with sport – hang gliding, extreme runs, bikes, bikes, bikes. They swam, they went to concerts, they studied at school, and for some reason, they were entranced by the only Irish bar in Annecy. There were plenty of Irish bars in my hometown in Lexington, Kentucky, because there were plenty of Irish, there for the horses. My staff made fun of me for sitting in bistros like all Americans in thrall with the French way of life, when I could go to an Irish bar, and was this not fun?

Leo, awake now and outraged at being left inside, scratched at the balcony door and ignored me when I told him to hush. I let him out and he stood beside me, and I kept a hand on his back as he searched the dark streets, and huffed, then barked sharply.

'Arrête,' I told him, then realized he saw what I had not.

Philippe on the corner, looking over his shoulder at two men who had come up behind him, and I caught his wary look in the glare of a shimmering streetlight. I clutched the railing. I could see anger in the set of my husband's shoulders, and I could see caution in how carefully he spoke to the men. I was afraid for him. I repositioned my aching ankle, scooting sideways so I could get to a place in the filigree railing to get a better view. Leo barked, deep chested and formidable, and the men looked back to our apartment. Philippe stood his ground; the conversation was short, unfriendly. Then the men disappeared down the dark rain-swept street. Philippe waved a hand at me. Or at Leo. It was hard to see. And then he walked away. I did not know where he was going.

I felt very alone, huddling on the wet deck of my little balcony, staring out into the dark, wet city. There were things going on with Philippe I did not know about – something to do with his work for the judge that he would not discuss. Or maybe something to do with the calls he had made.

I would wait up for him, to make sure he got home safe. I would not ask him why or what or who. I was afraid that he would lie – or worse, tell me the truth, and it would be something I was not yet ready to face.

ELEVEN

It was very late when Philippe came home to me. Leo barked and leaped off the bed when the apartment door opened. I heard Philippe talk to him softly. Waited while Philippe locked up, then stood in the bedroom doorway.

'You are awake?' he said softly.

I nodded.

'I have good news for you.' He came to the side of the bed, slipped his shoes off, slid out of the damp clothes, and curled up beside me. Careful of my ankle. Warm. I turned to face him, and he put an arm around me, kissed me quickly, and gave me a worried smile.

I wondered if his news really was good.

'Analise is safe for now, her baby is OK.'

'Stéphane—'

'Les Vipères Emeraudes returned him home to his farm. Analise. She is still in . . . captivity. Les Vipères Emeraudes rescued her too. That you know. But now they will not let her go. They say it is to keep her safe, but also, I think, she is useful to them right now.'

'How so? She's seven months pregnant, for God's sake, what happens if she goes into early labor?'

'They use her for publicity. A spin of the story. They are experts at that, you know this. It is Les Vipères Emeraudes who rescued her from the billionaire death squad, and Les Vipères Emeraudes who must keep her safe.'

'Even if she doesn't want to be kept safe?'

'Exactement. Why do you laugh?'

'Because I know Analise. They'll be sorry. And in the meantime, I'm going to find her and bring her home.'

'In truth, madame, I think I can help you with that.'

I sat up and looked at him. 'You know things?'

'I know things.'

So I had wronged him. He was not going to lie. 'What a useful husband you are.'

He smiled. He liked it when I noticed how great he was. He knew it but he liked me to know too.

'I saw those men. Who approached you in the street,' I said.

'Yes, Leo impressed them. I did not know you were there on the balcony.'

'Who were they?'

He shrugged.

'Is Madame Reynard involved in this?' I asked.

Madame Reynard was my nemesis. We were usually at odds. She ran a notorious and shadowy spy organization that flew under the banner of a climate change NGO, which was currently locked in a very public and ruthless, to-the-death feud with Sullivan Carr because of his plans to build a bitcoin mine on the pistes outside Annecy. Her fight against Carr was so personal that I wondered what Madame Reynard's real agenda was. Or perhaps I was misjudging her, and she just hated billionaires as much as I did. She was highly amused that VIE had forced her to up her game.

Madame Reynard had made it clear that she planned to make me useful, no matter how often I dodged her calls and meetings that she set up and I ignored.

'Madame Reynard?' Philippe said. 'I believe that she may have brought this trouble to you. She is putting pressure to bear on Sullivan Carr that we can only imagine. Much more than your website because she brings a lot to the table in terms of threats. She is deeply intwined with that world of power in government and for her Sullivan Carr . . . ce n'est pas la mer à boire—'

'Wait, what? No more than the sea to drink?'

'You would say the small potato. Like you she works for climate change, but her methods and her interests are a twist of influence and blackmail, and the flow of money is her domain. And if La Puce says Les Vipères Emeraudes have sent Carr the emerald of death, this means they will kill him for sure; they have the reputation to back this up.'

'And he comes after VIE instead? How is that fair.'

Philippe gave me a reluctant smile. 'This is not about fair. And you, my wife, are a pawn to be sacrificed for either side.'

'A pawn? A fucking *pawn*? This fucking pawn is going to take every one of them down.'

'I knew you would say that.'

'Have you spoken to Madame Reynard?'

He shook his head. 'She avoids me. She will know that she and I are at odds on this, but she thinks there is nothing I can do to her. She is circling The Emerald Vipers.'

'For or against?'

'Madame Reynard is never for or against. I believe that now she will do what she can to get a grip on them, so she can use them when she sees fit.'

'Are you going to tell me who you met with tonight?'

'I cannot. You understand?'

'I do, actually.'

'You are fâché?'

'No. I get it. It is OK if there are things you can't tell me. I just don't want you to lie.'

He touched my cheek. Smiled. 'Never.'

'Never is not true, Philippe.' I was bringing up a long-standing argument that we seemed unable to resolve, and I knew I should not hit him with this tonight, but when he said he'd never lie to me, it triggered a flash of annoyance.

He frowned at me. 'Are you once again going to bring up this ridiculous business about Oreo cookies?'

'You know this is not about Oreo cookies.'

'We will not discuss that tonight. And I am sorry, I forgot to bring you dinner.'

I turned on my back and stared up at the ceiling. 'I'm not hungry.'

'How is your ankle?'

'Do I have to be brave about this?'

'With me, madame?'

'It hurts like hell.'

He was asleep in minutes. I put my palm flat on his bare chest. He was sleeping deeply. Sleeping hard. And I heard that voice of wisdom in my head like a warning. *Appreciate this. Love him. You lived such agony when you lost Olivier. Hold on to what you have while you have it.*

These are the kind of thoughts that scare me. So full of relief. So laced with fear.

I laid my head on his shoulder. I didn't know what scared me the most. My future. Or my past. Remember the now, I decided. That will keep you out of the line of fire. The now is good, and that is all you need.

I wondered where Analise was sleeping tonight. I was sure that Stéphane was not sleeping at all.

I had no illusions about The Emerald Vipers. Analise had gone from the hands of one set of assassins to another, each with their own agenda. Sometimes I felt very small. Small and at war with the world.

But we were not helpless. They had not reckoned with Analise. With me. With VIE, and our citizen journalists all over the world. Our network of citizen spies.

Pissing off a billionaire was easy. Bringing a billionaire down was going to be a lot harder than I thought. And now I was in the crossfire of Sullivan Carr, Madame Reynard and Les Vipères Emeraudes. They would use me without conscience, without remorse. I would have to get smarter and use them.

TWELVE

The next morning, I mentally prepared myself to meet with the families of my young staff. They would want to know my version of what happened, and to discuss with me the funerals they would plan. I wondered if they blamed me. How could they not?

We had planned to meet in the private room of a restaurant one of the families owned. Even getting there felt formidable.

I hated the boot I had been given, and instead found a black, polyester brace in a drawer from my last ankle injury. I wore a thick sock beneath and laced it tightly enough for support. The ankle looked worse now the injury was taking hold. Bruising and swelling that disturbed me so much I decided not to look at it anymore.

The brace stabilized the joint and made my ankle hurt even more. The only shoes I could wear were high-top Converse trainers halfway unlaced, so flimsy and loose I could get my foot in them and not even scream.

The first thing I had to do was get myself and my dog out of the apartment and onto the street. Leo stayed close, reading my mind, sensing my fear, and that morning he had learned his new command. *Walk slow with Mama.* And he learned so quickly and with such eager affection that I knew that all would be well in my world if only I could get up and down the fucking stairs.

I began to think the definition of France was *stairs*.

Once on the streets, Leo matched his steps to mine and herded me to keep me on my feet, which had the opposite effect and sent me sideways more than once. There was no stifling the herding instinct of a Shepherd. So, I held on to things a lot.

The world looked different now. Curbs and cobblestones, broken pavement to navigate. People in a hurry, children running in and out of crowds like children do, some of them on scooters. Men on bikes who would run you down if you got in the way – in the way of cyclists who are wrapped in a world where bikes ruled. Mothers with massive strollers like torpedoes as they barreled forward, eyes only on their children. They wouldn't mean to make you grab the wall and hope not to be run over. They were just distracted and focused on the kids.

The population of Annecy is about one third canine, in my own personal estimation, which I like. Mostly they are leashed, and walking politely, though from time to time an unleashed dog will growl at another dog who passes too close, or go after one of the swans that are the pride of Annecy, and glide with elegance on the lake.

The dogs I could deal with, but the people were going to knock me on my ass.

I held tight to pillars and kept a hand on the sides of buildings.

When I arrived, Stéphane was already there. We felt a strange relief in each other's company, surviving together.

The families stayed grouped close together, in a loose, informal half circle of chairs, ready to listen as Stéphane and I gave our versions of what happened. They set the ground rules. Tell the truth, spare nothing; they needed to know. Anyone who did not want to listen to all of the details would discreetly leave the room.

No one did.

Stéphane and I went back and forth, he telling his part, me telling mine. He started with the woman at the barn, and we kept things in chronological order.

It was an ordeal to tell the story in a way that was the truth but shielded them from details I deemed not necessary for them to know. I noticed Stéphane doing the same. I could not get through it without tears and Stéphane was clearly numb and exhausted and burning hard with worry for Analise. I wanted to apologize to the families for putting the staff in danger, but I knew that this would mean the families would feel compelled to comfort me, and that is not why we were here.

For the first time I heard Stéphane's side of things – when we got to that moment in the hallway, when they led him away to his wife, and what he knew would be their death.

'She wasn't there,' Stéphane said. 'The man demanded she open the door to the bathroom, and when she did not respond, he kicked the door open. In the split second it took him to realize that Analise was not there . . .' He was executed with a shot to the head, and Stéphane made the acquaintance of a man who introduced himself as . . .

'La Puce?' I said.

There was a murmur from the families. The flea?

Stéphane nodded. 'He was very kind. He told me Analise was OK and had just been escorted out where they had taken down the wall.'

They told him to go quickly and quietly to the street, where someone would be waiting for him in a white Mercedes sedan. He did not think La Puce was police. But he was glad to get out alive. He thought – he'd been led to believe – that they were taking him to Analise, but they took him to his farm instead, told him that Analise was going to be kept in the protective custody of Les Vipères Emeraudes until 'things were safe'. He was given a business card and an apology written in fountain pen for their part in causing this incident. They wanted to assure him that they only had he and his wife's interests at heart.

He had refused to get out of the car until they took him to Analise. He was told this was not possible. He sat in the car for over an hour, refusing to get out, and they waited patiently, the driver telling him that he did not know where Analise was, but would be happy to wait until Stéphane was ready to face this.

Which he finally did. There were cows to be milked, and he believed the driver when he said he did not know where Analise was. And the sooner he reported it to the police, the better.

'Before I got out I asked him how I would know my wife was really safe, and he said she would do her first podcast. Tonight. I would hear her voice, and she would say what was happening with her, for the world to know she and our baby were safe and under their protection.'

'Tonight?' I asked.

'Yes,' he said. 'The usual time, seven PM.'

After we'd finished telling our truths, the families made decisions.

Three private funerals would be arranged, on coordinated days. And, at the request of all three families, VIE would hold a public memorial service at some time in the future. We were waiting for Analise to come home for that.

Hard as it was, meeting with the families had been good for me. To connect, to feel not judgment but the kind edge of their sorrow, and a strong sense that we were all in this together, and no one else could understand.

I was the last one out of the meeting. I stayed in case anyone had any questions or anything private to say. I received many kisses on the cheek.

The last person I talked to was Timothée's older sister, Lilou. She wanted me to know that she had decided to come and work for VIE.

She was a legend at the office. She had taught Timothée everything he knew, and he was very good, but Lilou was the genius. She told me she would take double her brother's salary and kissed me on both cheeks. She did not wait for me to agree.

THIRTEEN

That night, at seven PM, Analise Morel posted her first *Podcast in Captivity* on the VIE website. Philippe and I sat hand in hand on the couch, listening to it together.

Leo was better now. He was eating again. Sleeping upside down, and curled sideways, like a puppy.

Analise Morel sounded good. She sounded strong. She sounded very pissed off, and I thought that sooner or later The Emerald Vipers would give her back out of self-preservation.

Early yesterday morning, she said, a death squad was sent to VIE by a vulture capitalist billionaire who was unhappy with the reporting at VIE.

'We cannot yet name the attacker, but we can say that the police are looking very hard at "Daddy" Sullivan Carr. I was in the office bathroom when I heard screams, glass breaking, and gunshots. I locked myself in.

'Everything became quiet. There were no more screams.

'There is no window in the bathroom. I was afraid to leave. I am seven months pregnant with my first child.

'My computer was in my briefcase, and I tried to get help, but the internet in the office was down, and somehow I had lost my phone. I still have not found it.

'I heard noises in the hallway, and a small tap at the door. I was told by a man with a quiet, calm voice not to be afraid, and the door lock rattled, and then the door opened. The man had a rifle; he seemed very tough. He told me he was from Les Vipères Emeraudes and I would be under his protection. He told me I would be safe, but I must get out of the apartment fast.

'There was something about him . . . I believed him and that is why I am still alive today. He showed me where he had taken down part of the wall to the next apartment, told me to go through rapide, rapide, to the street below, and there would be a grey Mercedes waiting to take me to safety.

'But then I heard a voice from the front rooms. I knew it was my husband and I would not leave him, and the man said yes, my husband was there, and in great danger. I must go, he would make sure my husband was safe, he had just one more assassin to kill. I must get moving and let him do his job.

'So I did.

'I am safe with Les Vipères, this is true. But I want to go home. I have been told I must be protected, but they will not say how long for.

'I told them I have a job to do, and they made it possible for me to post this podcast.

'I believe VIE has been the target of for-hire assassins, a death squad sent by the billionaire Sullivan Carr. To prove such a thing, I will need your help. Soon I will be posting pictures of the assassins, provided by Les Vipères Emeraudes. Locations of where I think they have been, a crucial timeline. Les Vipères are helping me with this, but it is you, all of you, who watch and report back, who have the ability to prove what happened. In a world where we worry that dark shadowy powers are always watching us, and gathering information, we must remember that we can do the same, and there are more of us than them. Some of you will have seen things. Some of you will have pictures and videos. Help if you can.

'I wish to say two more things. Stéphane, my husband, I love you; our baby is OK. To the families of Timothée Fornier, Clementine Allard, and Louis Romilly. Je vous adresse mes sincères condoléances.

'I also wish to issue to everyone an invitation from Les Vipères Emeraudes. I do this of my free will, so that you will know they are calling for an extraordinary gathering on the Pont des Amours as we kick off our beautiful Venetian Carnival in Annecy, France. Details of time and place will be on our website.

'If it is in my power, I will talk to you soon.'

And then the music began. Analise played the song at the end of every podcast, a song about an upbeat, confident woman who does not want your riches; she wants your love. Zaz singing 'Je veux'. A song that was joyous, defiant, subversive . . . upbeat and irresistible.

'You are crying, madame.'

I smiled at Philippe. 'I don't know why, but I feel better.'

'Because she is alive. And like our Leo, she is always on the job.'

'And VIE is still in the fight. We are not alone, Philippe. We will be getting pictures, and sightings and we will find out things we need to know.'

'Along with the usual crap and harassment.'
'That goes without saying. And we are going to get our asses sued by Sullivan Carr.'
'The sun comes up; the sun goes down.' Philippe squeezed my hand.

But still, that night, I lay awake.
Philippe rolled over and pulled me close. 'You must sleep if you want that ankle to heal.'
'I feel like it's my fault.'
'Because you challenged a powerful, spoiled and dangerous man? No, madame, it is normal to feel that way, but this is not on you. Tout va bien passer.'
Everything will be fine. I needed him to say it. I might need him to say it forever.
'Capitaine Babineaux had a point, you know. Why didn't I call the police when I opened the envelope and saw the poster?'
'Do you think anyone has asked Stéphane Morel this question?'
I realized we were in one of those rare moments when Philippe was going to talk to me about real things. The podcast had shaken both of us up.
'I don't know. Why does it matter?'
'Junie. If I had opened that envelope and found that poster and thought you were in danger, I would have done exactly what you did and the world would have said yes, he is a man, he must protect his wife. And you, a woman, go to see to your staff, not knowing if this is real or harassment, you and Stéphane see broken glass on the pavement outside and run straight into danger and are almost killed. But still you go.
'We live in a world of misogyny, you know this. Do you think you can explain over the phone to police dispatch that you got a movie poster in an envelope and have thus concluded your staff is in danger and they must go tout de suite? That your star reporter may be killed by an angry billionaire? Not even I could make such a call and be believed. You would have been immediately routed to non-emergency and someone would have been assigned to do a welfare check. How long that would take, who knows?
'All of us, but women in particular – you grow up in a world where help sometimes does not come. Are you supposed to pace and worry and wish that things go OK, or do you take action?

'Regarde toi. I understand what it is to lay awake at night and second guess. I have many times wondered if I made the right call on the night of the Mont Blanc explosions.'

'Philippe. You saved the lives of your officers; you kept them out of danger from the explosives, because you knew to the inch how close they could get and be safe. The tunnel damage was just *stuff*.'

'The tunnel damage was money. If my officers had been killed and the tunnel not damaged, I would have gotten a medal and not lost my job.'

'Regrets?'

'No, madame. I would also have lost the man that I am. My point to you is we make the best decisions we can. You were brave, madame, and I love you for it, and worry about you for it too.'

And the weight of it lifted off my shoulders. The guilt, the blame, the second guessing.

'I don't think I can be mad at you about Oreo cookies anymore.'

He shut his eyes tight and sighed very loud. 'And this is over now? Finally? I have to say, madame, that I have become very tired of you refusing to come out to dinner with me, buying only Oreo cookies to eat, delivered box after box outside our door, filling up all the cabinet space, never shopping with me to buy actual food, refusing to ever cook again . . . why would you hold such a grudge?'

'Your son disrespected me in my kitchen.'

'How is it disrespect to eat an Oreo cookie? You made the beautiful brunch, and worked very hard, we had friends over, we were happy to see my son. If he says a thing that you do not like, why is it something we cannot ignore?'

His son had said the food was merde and had gone into the kitchen, come back with a package of Oreo cookies and eaten those instead.

'It was what *you* did that made me angry.'

'I told you nothing but the truth.'

'That children in France grow up eating Oreo cookies for breakfast and it was a natural thing for your son to do, and I just don't understand your culture?'

'Exactement.'

'I called your ex-wife.'

'Quoi?'

'I called your ex-wife and asked her if children in France grow up eating Oreo cookies for breakfast and it was a natural thing to do, and she said Oreo cookies were from America, and children in France had hot milk with chocolate in a bowl, and baguette for dipping, and whoever had told me this had told me a lie. So, it is not your son I am mad at – the children of divorce get upset and must work things out. No. The one I am mad at is you. You tell me a ridiculous lie—'

'*You called my ex-wife?*' He rolled over and pulled the blanket over his head.

'Philippe—'

'No more tonight, madame, I must sleep.'

I sat up and looked at him. 'Philippe. Do children in France eat Oreo cookies for breakfast?'

'Oui, madame. Tous les jours.'

Every day. Dammit.

FOURTEEN

When we first began targeting Sullivan Carr on VIE, I had naively expected the legal blowback of pissing off a billionaire to be the worst possible outcome. Death squads to take us down had never crossed my mind. Likely he would try again. Likely he would get me this time, unless The Emerald Vipers were quick on their feet. But evidently assassination was not enough.

Sullivan Carr began with the eviction of VIE from the apartment we rented for our office. Tenants' rights are strong in France, and sometimes the only way to remove a tenant is to sell the property. Carr had offered an astronomical sum to the British investor who had bought the apartment three years ago. Every other place in the building was an Airbnb. We had three months to vacate the premises.

Even in France, you can be evicted.

After a short in-person meeting, and a lot of clean-up and soul searching, we had decided to hold our ground and stay until the last possible moment. The bad memories would keep us sharp. In the meantime, I would look for a new place. Long-term rentals in Annecy were hard to come by.

We put pictures of all of us, living and deceased, on the wall. A memorial plaque had been ordered. The BILLIONAIRES SUCK banner had been rehung, proudly displaying three bullet holes. We felt tough. We felt brave. We felt defiant.

Timothée's sister was a perfect addition to the staff. She had mentored him, taught him everything he knew, and he had looked up to her, made fun of her, and had always gone to her for help and advice. He'd been awesome . . . but his sister was in another league. The first thing she proposed was a landing page on the website that kept track of billionaire retaliation. Sullivan Carr might get some blowback of his own.

But we were still in the crosshairs of a man whose wealth bought him pretty much everything he wanted. Death squads had been the first salvo of revenge.

Next came the lawyers. We would soon be in notaire and avocat hell.

Lawsuit one was a legal action against me from Olivier's family, who had never welcomed me with open arms. They were making a claim on his estate, which had already gone through probate in the US. It was a bullshit move and the Paris attorney I hired felt this was a harassment lawsuit and required deep pockets to file.

While Olivier's mother, sister, and brother had jointly filed the lawsuit, their choice of representation was a high-rolling Swiss firm based in Geneva – on retainer with Sullivan Carr.

Once the Alpine bitcoin mine was in play, Sullivan Carr had had the honor of being the first billionaire Analise featured in VIE's podcast *Billionaires Behaving Badly*.

For me, the choice had been personal. Carr was not good for Annecy, and he was not good for my home state of Kentucky.

The EU and Kentucky were becoming enthusiastic trade partners on a massive scale of escalating billions. The state of Kentucky now had a European office, whose website said: *Welcome to Kentucky, Your New American Home.*

Kentucky was now well on the way to implementing strict EU regulations, energy-efficient green technology, and everybody was minting money because renewable energy was not just good for the world, it was profitable as hell, though the oil and gas companies and Sullivan Carr himself would tell you otherwise.

The high standards of the EU were welcomed in Kentucky and the EU was delighted – they could not reach their global climate change goals alone. But while the governor of Kentucky was taking meetings in Germany and Switzerland and they were all drinking the bourbon, the name Sullivan Carr had begun to come up.

It was not a good look for Kentucky – a home-grown mega billionaire claiming massive carbon credits in the Amazon for land he did not actually own or manage. A typical billionaire scam. The majority of his investments were in fossil fuels, and agribusiness. He had the usual massive carbon footprint of a billionaire with his private jets and hungry energy consumption. He'd paid zero income taxes for the last three years, according to an investigation by ProPublica.

And now he was trying to muscle a bitcoin mine into the French alps. His reason? Nobody yet had figured that out. In truth, it was the *only* part of his financial holdings that did not bother the movers and shakers of business between Kentucky and France.

Who did it bother? It bothered the people who lived near them. It bothered the wildlife. The dirty emissions bothered the actual Earth. It sure as hell bothered VIE.

Carr also owned a horse farm on Iron Works Pike in Lexington, used a shady, unloved and high-profile trainer whose horses had a shocking fatality rate, bred for speed over soundness, and this caused a lot of local outrage. He and his trainer refused to let female jockeys ride their horses, and his biggest goal in life right now was to win the Kentucky Derby. No matter how spoiled the billionaire, that was a goal that was usually out of reach. This year, Carr's chances looked pretty good.

Once Analise and I discussed the issue of Carr's racehorses breaking down, the choice of our first billionaire to go after had been a no-brainer and there was no stopping us. She had a gelding named Cooper who owned her heart, and I was still mourning the death two years ago of my beautiful Empress, a registered National Show Horse, which is an Arab-Saddlebred mix.

Of all the things Sullivan Carr had done, it was the horses that made us go after him so hard.

What I did not tell Analise was that I had history with Carr's son by wife two, one Clifton Carr, who liked to refer to himself as Gatsby. Gatsby was the child of Carr's heart, though he spent most of his time with mistress three, who had also had a Sullivan Carr son, who was more of a rumor than a presence in Kentucky. The word *vasectomy* was known to set Carr off in a rage, and there were tales told of far-flung progeny. No doubt Carr's wealth managers were keeping track.

Gatsby was spoiled, which went without saying – drug and alcohol fueled but only on the weekends – and was considered the most highly prized party guest in town. To his credit, he was good at partying and practiced a lot. He was also passionate about winning bids for massive downtown development projects, but not as interested in actually getting them done, and a Clifton Carr Kentucky Development deal had become something of a local joke.

Gatsby and my brother had enjoyed a tumultuous year of love and rage a decade ago, and the biggest feud between the two of them was who had jilted who. I knew the truth. I had been the stalwart sister back then, and my brother's heart had been well and truly broken.

The bitterness between them had eventually simmered to medium cool and now they were almost friends. Gatsby had been intrigued by my brother's husband, Redmond, and upon meeting him in the actual flesh had donned his reading glasses and asked Redmond to spin in a circle so he could inspect all of him. Redmond had walked away. My brother had laughed and said, 'Hands off my husband.' Gatsby had sent the two of them a case of Angel's Envy bourbon, and open hostilities had finally ceased. Evidently, I was the only one still holding a grudge.

But not about my brother.

My dispute with Gatsby involved a horse. That little Arab mare named Empress. Brought in cross country from Wisconsin, and arriving on a Sallee horse van on a chill but sunny October day. Everyone at the barn had gone out front to see her, this glossy, chestnut mare with perfect conformation. She had been brought in to compete and was known for a beautiful action that won her first place if her rider could stay on her back.

Registered name – *First Empression*. Foaling date – *20 April*. Sire – *R B Aquila*. Dam – *Briguetta*. Star, strip and snip over right nostril to right upper lip. Left hind sock. Freeze mark on left side of neck. Percentage Arabian Blood – 75%.

Gatsby had taken one look at her, trembling and exhausted, robust and compact at not quite fifteen hands high, and had taken a whim to be unimpressed and backed out of the sale. She was small and elegant and very afraid, and he had dismissed her with a shrug and a sneer. In truth he had a point. He was on the large side for a horse that size.

I was there the day that Empress was led off the truck, and from the moment I saw her she captured my heart. I knew this horse, like a future memory.

I went straight to the barn manager who had put the deal together and was royally pissed because Gatsby had backed out. She sold Empress to me for the price of transport . . . $2,500. A sweetheart deal but she knew she'd make good money on the back end – charging me a lowered monthly board fee, in exchange for letting her competition riders show Empress, who was a phenomenon in the ring. She would sell me expensive riding lessons that I very much wanted; I would pay board, and all expenses, and Empress would bring prestige to the barn. That's how horse business is done.

Gatsby realized his mistake soon enough.

To the extreme annoyance of everyone in the barn, I had decided to show Empress myself. There was no competition Empress would lose if I could stay on her back, though not getting killed was always job one. She was way over my pay grade, and I loved her with all my heart, and though she loved me too, she would spin, and bolt, and panic, and flighty did not even begin to describe her level of fear.

Even the good riders in the barn, who tried to show me what's what with my own horse, would get off her back a little tight lipped and pale, and nobody rode her more than once.

Her nickname in the barn was The Maserati.

The offers to buy her came discreetly. Other riders did not want to compete against her, and there were a lot of noses in the air, rightly making the point that my riding was barely competent, but the horse was first rate. She should go to somebody who would be worthy of the horse.

I turned away all offers and doubled down. I refused to let anyone else at the barn ride or show her, and got my board fee upped substantially when I took her off the circuit. She was an unhappy horse. Full of nerves and anxiety. I had no idea what I was doing, but I wanted to give her a break and figure that out.

When word got out that Gatsby was actually the one trying to buy her back, there was a great deal of nasty amused gossip. Barn politics are hell, no matter how much money you had.

I had been inexperienced and an obvious mark for the barn manager to milk for money, dazzled by my love for horses, and eager to learn. She was shocked and outraged the day the Sallee van arrived and I took Empress out of the barn, and she predicted in a fury that the horse would kill me someday.

I never looked back. You learn as you go. I had a horse I loved. My mare and I figured things out on our own.

FIFTEEN

When I next saw Le Sorcier, the assassin who did not go for cut-rate prices, he was walking down the sidewalk toward me with a look of utter delight. I knew that he had been stalking me, taking note of my habits. And he had caught me alone without Leo.

More and more I was leaving Leo home.

The two of us had managed to navigate the apartment stairs by letting him off leash to go ahead of me, while I slid down step by step on my ass. Once we were on the sidewalk, he had learned to match his steps to mine, and the offbeat cadence of my massive limp. But I was off balance, holding onto walls and posts because too often the world went sideways with no warning. I developed a great appreciation for the metal barricades that cordoned off parts of the streets while they were under 'traffic calming' construction, some being fully converted to pedestrian traffic.

But Annecy was full of people in a hurry, and they pushed and pressed too close. Twice Leo had a close call with men on bikes, and once with a six-year-old on a scooter. I was afraid of falling; I could not move fast enough to keep him safe, and he would not hesitate to get between me and anything coming toward us.

And so I was heading toward Monoprix alone, where there were sweaters on sale. I'd bought a black turtleneck two days ago and liked it so much I was going to buy another one. When I love a sweater, I like to have two.

Le Sorcier was rounding the corner on Rue Joseph Blanc and I was headed across the street after lunch at Bon Pain Bon Vin. He gave me a big smile, frowned, shaking his head and looking down at my swollen left foot, encased in the ankle brace and my dirty old Converse shoes. He gave me a troubled look, the only off thing the intensity in his eyes. A sort of excitement now that he had his prey firmly in hand, a look of deep concern on his face that I would swear was genuine.

'Madame, you are in pain.'

I was in pain. Quite a lot of pain.

He grabbed both of my hands, kissing them, then pulled me close and kissed both of my cheeks. He was inches away. Smiling with eyes on fire.

'The ankle is broken?'

'No.' I pulled back, but he held me in place.

'Surgery?'

I shook my head.

He tilted his head to one side. 'A very bad sprain, then. That will take even longer to heal than a break. I am sad to tell you, madame, that unless you rehab this ankle with constancy and care, it will never be the same.'

He pulled me in to his chest, leaving no space between us, wrapped me in a tight hug, and it was all I could do to stay on my feet. To hug a woman on the streets in France was not done, and that shocked me more than the gun I felt beneath his leather jacket. I pushed backward, leaning against the long wide window of Monoprix. There were people inside who gave us a second look, and he stepped back.

'My ankle is going to be better than before,' I told him. 'You've been hurt, in your line of work. You know these things can heal.'

'My line of work, madame?' He still had my hands.

'Assassin.'

He laughed. 'Most people do not say that to my face, with the exception of my father, who is a son of a bitch, but very proud. I have thought lately for a career change. He will not be happy with me, but he so rarely is.' He tilted his head to one side. 'Since you ask. First you soak the ankle in hot water and salt, for fifteen minutes. While you do that, have a wet towel in the freezer and when you finish soaking in hot water, wrap the cold towel around the ankle, you see? Ten minutes for the cold. And now listen to me, because the next step is very important. Put a few drops of olive oil on your palms and massage the ankle gently for eight minutes like this.' He rubbed his hands together just so, and I admit the technique looked good. 'Afterward . . .' He put his head sideways on folded hands. 'Dormez. You must sleep, it is the only way the ankle will heal.'

'Your English is excellent, but your accent is very French. Where are you from?'

'I am from everywhere and nowhere.'

'Did you read that in a book?'

He sighed. 'I had a French mother and a tiresome American father. *Your* French, by the way, needs some work.'

'I am studying. Laissez-moi. You understand that? *Let go of me.*'

'I will decide when to let go of you and I am not ready yet.' He turned my hands up for more kisses, this time on the soft pinkness of my palms.

I lifted his hand to my lips and bit him very hard, tearing flesh and drawing blood, which I spat into the street at his feet.

He gave me a look of shock and laughed. 'Compliments on drawing first blood.'

'What, you think you're breaking new ground here, threatening a woman on the street? Because women deal with men like you every day of their lives, and you are old news.'

He gave me a sideways look. He enjoyed playing with me, that was clear. A twisty form of assassin flirt. Let us have banter and smiles before I blow your head off.

'To business, madame. I have a proposal for you from my employer.'

'Him again. I don't want to hear this.'

He held my wrists hard. 'You will listen. What you must do is this. You will post on your website that new evidence shows the attack on VIE came from the terrorist group Les Vipères Emeraudes. That Sullivan Carr has been in touch with VIE and it has been proven that the Vipers have been manipulating VIE for publicity as well as threatening Carr with the delivery of a small emerald, which is a sentence of death from this group. And that is true, Junie, they have done this. You will say that Carr is a gentleman who has shown the proper concern, as well as making a generous donation to the cause. Also – stop posting the Bigfoot protests of the bitcoin mine.'

'Dude. No.'

'You must know by now that you never say no to a billionaire.'

'And you must know by now that is the whole point of VIE.'

'Listen to me, madame. You wish to live? You wish to enjoy your life in this country you seem to love so much with your oh-so-handsome husband? You have no idea how vulnerable you are, with or without your dog.' He gave me a half smile. 'I can hurt you or I can help. Truly I can help. Use your NGO and VIE for climate change recycling advice, but let go of your billionaire obsession.'

'You do know that recycling is a fucking scam?'

He closed his eyes tight for one moment. Then gave me a serious look.

'Then choose another billionaire. Think how it will be to feel safe once again, to have the avocats and notaries called off, because trust me, the lawsuits are only just beginning. Don't you want your lease for VIE restored? Have you ever looked for a rental in this town? Think how wonderful it would be to let the nightmare of these last few days fade.' He waved a hand. 'So. I will not give him that message, because if I do, he will escalate, so I will give you some time to reconsider. Do it soon, he has the patience of a child, which is no patience at all, and next time you won't see me coming.'

'I've heard that about you.'

'Believe it. For now, just for today, I will give you a pass and will not kill you by slitting your throat and letting you bleed out here on this beautiful street. If you know your history, you will understand that blood on cobblestones is not unheard of in France.'

He cupped my chin in his hands, blood drying on his wrist, and kissed my cheeks, and we looked into each other's eyes like lovers, his gaze locked with mine. And then he let me go and took a step back.

'I will have your answer in, say, forty-eight hours?'

'You can have my answer now. Because unlike Sullivan Carr, I don't have to win. I just have to make him sorry. And I'm making *good* progress on that. We're going to double down and go after him harder. And call it revenge if you want, because that is just another word for accountability, and accountability – that's what VIE is all about. *Holding billionaires accountable.* And there are more of us than there are of them. We've had a stream of job applications since VIE was attacked. Kill me and the problem continues, because there will always be someone to take my place. Either way, your billionaire is going to lose.

'So, you give Sullivan Carr a message from me. Run for your life, hide out in your bunker, go to Mars on a spaceship with Elon Musk. Because the Green Vipers are coming, and from what I've seen of them, it's going to be a hardcore takedown. And I will be waiting and I will be watching, and if the Green Vipers don't kill him, I promise you, *I will*. He won't see it coming, and it *is* going to hurt.'

Le Sorcier froze and studied me. I could see the grey in the three-day growth of beard, and the chestnut brown of his hair. And

I knew the light in his eyes meant he was rethinking. Perhaps instead of letting me go, he might just get on with it after all. One more casualty for VIE.

There were people suddenly, a little knot of them talking and leaving the little bistro across from Monoprix, and one of them noticed us and stopped. The assassin glanced over my shoulder and the light went out of his eyes.

And I knew two things. That if he was trying to intimidate me, it was working; and that he had not just had a gun tucked away, but a knife in the sleeve of his very expensive black leather jacket that fit him loosely, not as tailored as mine.

I headed away down the sidewalk, limping and slow, running a hand along the side of the building to stay on my feet, and turned left around the corner, and disappeared into Monoprix. I passed the security guard in the doorway, and threaded randomly through the shelves, wondering how much it hurt to have your throat slit, and how long it would take to die. Maybe I would research that later.

Maybe not.

I looked out the plate-glass windows, heart pounding, hands shaking, to see if Le Sorcier was out still there, to see if he was close. I wandered past make-up, yogurt and prepared lunches, back to the sweaters, and did not see him.

Better to go while I could. I wasn't far from the apartment, something he would know. I knew I would be doing exactly as expected, but it didn't stop me. I wanted to go home.

It was a long, careful climb up the stairs to my apartment, to Leo.

I needed to get my ankle healed; I did not like being trapped against a wall unable to run. Tomorrow I would go to the pharmacy and ask for strengthening exercises and lavender Epsom salts, and I would stop at L'Occitane en Provence for lavender cream.

I hugged Leo, then did forty minutes of careful, gentle yoga, soaked my ankle in hot water, wrapped it in an icy towel, then massaged it with olive oil, which made me sigh.

Le Sorcier had given excellent advice. The olive oil seemed to pull the inflammation and ease the ache; my ankle felt better now than it had since I had hurt it. I pulled on a pair of thick white socks and avoided looking at the swelling and the black bruising that streaked along the side of my foot like a Nike logo and gave me a queasy feeling. I decided to do this twice a day, the yoga, the soaking, the olive oil. I would do it before and after I played my guitar, in the morning and at night. Ankle injuries were not just painful, they were time consuming.

I curled up on the couch and went to sleep, Leo tucked up at the end of the couch, head on my good leg, my bad ankle propped up on a pillow.

SIXTEEN

I slept long and hard, and woke when I heard Philippe talking softly to Leo. Evidently Philippe had come home, taken Leo out for a short walk, and now Leo was demanding play time, and the squeak of the toy and the thunder of paws even I could not sleep through. I put the blanket over my head.

'Your mama, she does not want to wake up.' Philippe peeled the blanket off the top of my head and smiled at me. 'You drink wine and sleep in the afternoon?'

'No, just the sleep. I have not touched a glass of wine since I hurt my ankle. My balance is off. I need to keep my head clear.'

He nodded. His smile faded. 'You are fâché?'

'Angry? Yes. But not with you.'

'That at least is good.'

'Something happened this afternoon.'

He waited. And I wondered if I should tell him or keep it to myself. I was pulling away from him, and I knew it.

'Leo needs to be fed.' I sat up, and he grabbed my hand.

'What happened this afternoon?'

I shrugged. 'I'll handle it.'

'Then let me tell you. You were walking to Monoprix, yes? After you had your lunch. And you left Leo at home because three times now he has almost been hurt in the streets. And this one known as Le Sorcier, he came around the corner, talking and looking at you with such eyes.'

'Scary eyes.'

'Yes. And he took your hands and kissed both of your cheeks and hugged you in the street and held you hard when you tried to pull away. And you kept backing up till you were against the wall.'

That part I did not remember.

'And he talked to you and you shook your head, and you bit him. It made me smile to hear that. And you talked a while, and then La Puce decided to intervene and he walked in the street to let this one see him, which is all he needed to do.'

'That is why he let me go? La Puce was there?'

Philippe nodded.

'Would he have—?'

'No. This was his time to figure you out, and to frighten you. If he had wanted to kill today, believe me, you would be dead. La Puce thinks Le Sorcier has been told to watch you, openly, to make you afraid. To kill you now would be very bad publicity, but if you keep going after Carr like you do, they may decide to go that way.'

'It's working. He scared me. He had a knife; I could feel it under his sleeve.'

Philippe gave me a worried look. 'He does not need a weapon, that one. He likes to . . .' He trailed off. Shrugged.

I waited. I decided I didn't want to know.

'God, this is a small town.'

'Les Vipères Emeraudes are watching you, more than you know.'

'Yes, I understand they are big fans of VIE. So at least I have friends.'

Philippe shook his head. 'No, madame. They find you useful. Do not take them for *friends*; they would sacrifice you without hesitation if it suited their cause. They are dangerous, these men and women; they are everywhere, you do not know where they will be, and if they turn on you, they will be worse than Le Sorcier.' He took both my hands. 'I am sorry he scared you today.'

I closed my eyes. Nodded. I did not like to admit such things. Next would come the part where he told me not to worry and everything would be OK.

'I do not like him grabbing you that way in the street.'

Typical Frenchman. *Do not hug my wife.*

'How is your ankle?' Philippe peered down at my foot, reaching to turn it to one side.

'Don't touch it.'

'This seems very swollen and it worries me that you hold it sideways like that. Why are you not wearing the boot?'

'It throws me off balance, it keeps my leg locked in one position, and if I wear that thing and I fall, I won't be able to maneuver, and I am going to get *really* hurt.'

'Where is it now?'

'I threw it off the balcony.'

'I will go and get it.'

'I'm not wearing it, Philippe.'

'We cannot leave it in the street, madame. If your ankle is no better, we should get it looked at again.'

'It is better. Le Sorcier gave me good advice on how to rehab this with olive oil.'

'He is strange, that one. La Puce tells me he has patterns and rituals. And when he makes the kill, he shaves his head, and his face, and wears a white shirt, and black wool trousers, which he destroys later. There is ritual in his method and some common sense.'

'What is this thing, with you and La Puce? How do you know him so well?'

'Ah, that one? He is formidable.'

'Funny, he says the same thing about you.'

I wondered about this wariness La Puce and Le Sorcier had of my husband. It was a reality shift for me. That Philippe had a certain notoriety for being relentless and tough in law enforcement circles, I knew. But this other thing. This reputation he had of being formidable if you fucked with him. I had not seen that side of him, that he kept out of our marriage. He had said to me one night with a slow and weary smile that I was high maintenance and had no idea how often he protected me when I was unaware, and I had laughed and not believed him.

I believed him now.

'Madame, if your ankle is better, I am thinking of where we can go to dinner.'

I had not had dinner out with Philippe since the Oreo Cookie War began.

'Also, I must ask you. There are two more delivery boxes of Oreo cookies at the bottom of the stairs. Will you please make this stop?'

'I canceled the orders, but those were already in transit.'

'We have no room in this apartment for all of my shirts, much less all of these Oreo cookies. I propose a plan. I will have them delivered to my son.'

It made me laugh.

'Let us go to L'Atlas, ça va? You will come.'

'I will come and we will take Leo. You will help me keep him safe.'

'We will put him between us.' He looked at me steadily. With a slow smile. We were finding our way back to each other; he knew it and so did I. 'And you will have the mussels like you always do?'

'And you will have the steak tartare.'

'Please, this once you will try it?'

'Never in a million years. Unless—'

'You negotiate with me? What is it I must do?'

'Tell me everything about Les Vipères Emeraudes. You know a lot of things you aren't telling me.'

I could not read the look on his face.

'Please accept that I have told you a lot already, and for now that is all I can say.'

'But you will send the cookies to your son?'

'That, I promise, madame. We are being overrun.'

SEVENTEEN

Dinner between us was tense, and I was not sure why. Philippe had not been playful at dinner or asked me to sample the steak tartare or teased me about it, like he usually did.

But then he took my hand across the table, gave it a squeeze, and I thought he was finally ready to talk. He looked at me steadily, in a way that let me know he was worried, and I saw the cop, the man, the husband. Thinking, making decisions about what he would tell me. All the happy pleasure I had felt at being out once again for dinner with my husband, drained away.

'You know things,' I said softly.

L'Atlas was winding down for the night. There were two other people at a table on the other side of the restaurant, and Philippe had ordered a second bottle of wine. A local white, not too sweet, and with a buttery smoothness that was light and an utter pleasure to drink. It is something that you only find in the local wines of the Haute-Savoie.

He refilled my glass.

'Junie, the things I know can get you killed.'

I put my wine glass down and waited. 'More killed than already? Tell me, Philippe.'

'You must give me time to think.'

'You're afraid of what I will do? When you tell me your secrets?'

'Always, madame.'

'This is not a chess game, Philippe.'

'Oh yes, madame, it is. Chess is war, and so is this.'

EIGHTEEN

Philippe slept with his arms around me that night. He did not let me go. I envied his ability to sleep no matter what. I did not sleep at all. I wanted this over, but things kept getting worse and worse. I would not back down, but evidently, neither would I sleep.

The next morning Philippe was up early, as he always was. I heard the shower. Then the bubble of coffee in the old Moka pot. He crept quietly into the bedroom to set a tiny cup of hot coffee on the bedside table, leaned over me, and kissed me on the cheek like he did every morning before he left.

Today he did not leave. Today he sat on the side of the bed. 'You are pretending to be asleep.'

'Tell me what you know,' I said softly.

He waited a moment, gave up, and went to work.

I poured the coffee down the sink, rinsed out the cup.

There were children sitting on a bench beside the canal across from my window. And Mont Blanc, solid, behind them. No snow on the mountain, no snow in Chamonix. There is less and less snow every year, and the glaciers are melting away. The mountain a patchwork of bare rock and deep green.

The canals in front of Le Pâquier park were lined with boats, one upturned and covered in algae. The rest of them were upright, securely tied, moving gently in the water and the wind. The boats were white, the interiors blue. Across the park I could see the lake, ripples of teal and midnight blue, rivulets and waves running strong, to lap at the rock of the mountain on the other side.

The mountain was my anchor. Almost everywhere I went in Annecy I could see it. I was uneasy when I couldn't, relieved when I turned a corner, and there it was again. Solid and safe. My compass, because even in Old Town, I could get lost from one twisting street to the next, which astounded Philippe to no end.

From this distance away the mountain was security, but up close and personal, Mont Blanc was the most dangerous mountain in the world. I was a veteran of the Smoky Mountains in Tennessee, where hiking was like slogging through a rainforest. And of the blocky bare mountains outside of Atlanta, Georgia. Memories of living there as a very little girl, spending a weekend with my family in North Carolina, riding a little mountain train, and getting the square red sticker that said I RODE TWEETSIE. Putting it on the headboard of my bed, looking at it every single day for years.

Philippe was working long hours in Metz these days and would not be home till late. He refused to sleep over. 'I will be with you tonight,' he told me. 'Quite late, so have your dinner.'

'I'll wait till you come back.'

I could not settle. Not to my guitar, my dog, or my kitchen. I slid into my black leather jacket, professionally cleaned of blood, softer, with shadows of stains in the leather that would never go away. I wrapped a slate-blue scarf around my neck. Gloves and a hat, it was chilly, and I would walk as long as my ankle let me, then sit for a while on a bench. Leo was up on his feet. Ready to go out. We had been too much inside.

It was good to be out of the apartment. I sure as hell did not want to go back home. Nor did I want to go to the office, which was full of defiant energy, work, worry and threat. The memory of carnage on the floor, and a reality shift into shock.

I would go anyway. I kept my second-best guitar there. If I could not concentrate, I would sit in my leather armchair and play. High time I reclaimed my space. I had to have somewhere to go, in spite of billionaires and husbands.

I told myself it would be fine. I told myself it would be good. We had, after all, cleaned up all of the blood. But before I made it to the office, I saw him for the first time. The man in black. The Marquis.

NINETEEN

I had just turned the corner of Rue du Lac when I saw him for the first time. A masked man in black, wearing the Venetian costume of the Marquis, though the carnival had not yet begun. I wondered just for a moment if he was real, so softly and silently did he glide, watching me from across the street. A town this old sees many ghosts.

And this one was elegant, very focused on me, moving quickly. Leo was watchful, but quiet. Leo had not allowed anyone with a mask to approach me during his first carnival, but he seemed now to take it in stride. Another year older, and a carnival veteran now.

This Marquis swept off his hat and bowed very deeply. Chrome metal mask. Elegant black jacket of thick velvet, trimmed in gold with leather buttons, nipped at the waist and falling to his thighs. Loose breeches in cognac, buttoned beside each knee, and tall, below-the-knee black boots with heavy gold buckles. Chamois gloves, and a snow-white ruffled cravat. Silk gloves, a tricorn black hat trimmed in gold with a cognac plume. The rigidity of his shoulders loosened, the stoic look had disappeared, and I saw he was smiling beneath the mask. He had a square strong jaw. Masculine.

This was a normal interaction during carnival. Men and women in Venetian costume, weaving their way through the city, stopping for pictures, a bow, a hand raised. The Venetian Carnival players.

He settled the hat back in place, stared at me the way some Frenchmen do. My eyes first, then the sweep, down my body, and back up again, meeting my eyes yet again. Taking his time over it, this one. Insolent. I stood my ground.

The man crossed the street toward me, and Leo alerted me with a huff. The Marquis hesitated, then moved at an angle to the sidewalk. Reached inside his jacket and brought out a small paper-wrapped bouquet of tiny, delicate, white bell-shaped flowers nestled in emerald-green leaves. Lilies-of-the-valley – muguets.

During the Renaissance, King Charles IX would present lilies-of-the-valley to the ladies of the court, when the flowers bloomed in May, a good luck charm. It became an official holiday on May

1st, 1941, la Fête du Muguet. Lily-of-the-valley day. A man who did not bring such a bouquet to the woman he loved was a man in hot water. A gesture of affection and good luck, a symbol of springtime and renewal. But in France, May 1st was also about labor rights and social movements. Solidarity with the USA. For Les Vipères Emeraudes, the symbolism would be impossible to resist. Charm, a flirt, and a political point. That about summed them up, when they were not sending an assassin to your door. I wondered where they got the flowers, so early in the year.

I held my hand out for the bouquet, the man nodded, and came close, a wary eye on Leo, whose collar I held tight.

The softness of his chamois gloves lightly brushed the skin between my jacket and my red leather glove, and I looked up to see him smile, eyes watchful beneath the mask. Then he turned swiftly and disappeared in a twist of the street.

I unwrapped the paper around the bouquet and saw that it was one of the fliers that had been plastered all over the city, right after the blood-drenched attack on VIE, causing a stir of anxiety, talk, and excitement. The attack, the Vipers, the fliers – it was all over the news, covered internationally, and the speculation had reached a fever pitch within a twenty-four-hour news cycle.

The reactions were all over the place. The carnage at VIE, in a gentle town that did not welcome the speculation, the manipulation of press pundits and politicians and journalists. The Tragedy Tourism that was seeping in.

The gentle elegant carnival had been hijacked by violence and politics. And I had my hand-delivered invitation.

I loosened my grip on Leo, moved off the sidewalk, and read the flier, puzzling over the French.

Les Vipères Emeraudes would be on the world-famous bridge, the Pont des Amours, at midnight on day one of the carnival. There an announcement would be made, for everyone in Annecy to hear. For everyone *in the world* to hear.

> Friends, and people of Annecy. For those of you who are sick in heart, to see the blood of your citizens splashed in the streets, to see the beauty of the Glières plateau, where our own resistance took a stand against the fascists in 1941, destroyed by a bitcoin mine and a billionaire. Know this.

The nightmare has returned and the nightmare will be stopped.

Join us. Be there on our own Bridge of Love, where we will take a stand, and cut the heads off the ones that will take our city, our freedom, and our land.

Do not stand by. Stand together, my friends. We meet at midnight precisely.

This flier had my name on it, in heavy thick black marker. You will be there, Junie Lagarde. We will keep you safe.

I already had Le Sorcier on my ass, courtesy of billionaire Daddy Carr. And now the Vipers would be following me, anonymous in masks and costume, slipping through the crowds when I crossed a street, sitting across from me at a cafe, fading into the background while they watched me.

I was to see them again and again, the Venetian Vipers. Different heights, different builds, different costumes, different masks. But all of them watching me, staying close.

I had Viper bodyguards to keep me safe. So long as I did what I was told.

I would take the bouquet to the office. We had a decision to make.

TWENTY

Outside of the office, the broken glass on the sidewalk had been swept away. Bouquets of flowers had been laid next to the building, some fresh, some turning dry and brown. It meant the world to me. Like we were not so alone.

Inside, the office was teeming with energy when Leo padded ahead of me through the door. Timothée's sister, Lilou, was in the little kitchen where her brother had died. I would never again be able to think of it as just *the kitchen*. She was a force of nature, like Analise Morel on steroids.

'Bonjour, Junie, salut.'

Like her brother, Lilou wore heavy motorcycle boots, but unlike him she rode a hot-pink scooter, would not wear a helmet, and left her boots just inside the front door as soon as she arrived. She refused to wear them at work because boots interfered with her concentration. Her daily uniform was black tights and oversized white dress shirts, with a soft, cognac suede belt with a big gold buckle that she wrapped twice around her waist. Her hair was collar length, straight and soft, a deceptively simple but expensive cut.

There were only two meals she would eat. Fried rice with vegetables, or spinach sauteed in olive oil and balsamic vinegar, with sundried tomatoes and aged parmesan cheese. Sometimes she would add eggs to sauté with the spinach. She made more use of the kitchen than anyone else at VIE.

I had brought two delivery boxes of Oreo cookies to the office, and it was oddly gratifying that she opened herself to a third choice – Oreo cookies for lunch. 'But never for breakfast,' she assured me, lifting her head over the baffling cocoon of equipment she was setting up. Computers, servers, wires and wires and wires.

The Oreo Cookie War with Philippe was legend with my staff.

'There are things we must discuss,' she said, wandering out of the kitchen with a small coffee.

I settled into one of two brown leather IKEA armchairs in front of the balcony, and Leo settled into the other one. 'Let's call an impromptu meeting of the staff. Who's here?'

'Nous tous.' All of us.

She trotted up and down the hallway, shouting, 'Réunion immédiate, allez, on se bouge, les gars.'

Meeting right now. Let's go. Move it, guys.

For France, this apartment was big, and shouting up and down the hallways had become the VIE communication style. My staff was young. Lyam, not quite thirty, solid build, smirky, and our open-source researcher, trotted down the hall right behind her, and after he settled, Lilou began to bring us up to date.

I looked down the hallway. 'Isn't Matis here?' Matis was the most junior member of the staff.

'Aux chiottes,' Lyam said. In the toilet. He settled into the kind of tube and chrome chair favored by everyone but me.

Lilou shrugged and sat on the edge of her desk. 'We must look at these pictures I have gathered together and decide what we post.'

The call for help Analise had made in the first episode of *Podcast in Captivity* had brought in pictures, videos and sightings of the death squad duo who had attacked VIE. You cannot wander through a smallish city full of tourists in military flak jackets without getting a second look. A lot of non-locals had assumed they were police.

We liked the shot of the woman and the man standing on the corner outside VIE, time stamp fifteen minutes before the shooting began. One of broken glass on the sidewalks, emergency vehicles, police. And one of Le Sorcier, back to the camera, embracing me in front of Monoprix.

Lyam gave a low whistle. 'That one can be taken a lot of different ways. Should we even put it up?'

'Full disclosure,' I said. 'Always. We need Matis. I want to know how soon we can get these vetted and ready to go.'

A toilet flushed.

Lyam smirked as Matis came thundering into the living room. 'Eh. Le chef wants to know how long before we get the new pictures and videos up.'

'By the end of the day.' Matis, not a day over twenty, grinned at me. 'We will put Sullivan Carr in his place. Il pète plus haut que son cul.'

I frowned and Lyam waved a hand at Matis. 'Translation for le chef.'

'It means he is arrogant, Junie. Strict translation – he farts higher than his backside.'

'Give me a minute, I want to write that down.'

'Can we put it on the website?' Matis said. 'Maybe as a descriptive sort of definition of billionaires—'

'Non,' Lilou said.

Lyam shook his head.

'Children,' I said. 'Behave.'

'One other thing we're getting,' Lyam said. 'Job applications. Everyone wants to work here now.'

'I thought no one would touch us after . . .' I trailed off. 'Send them to me. We need to staff up.'

'There are a lot.'

'Sort them for the serious and the qualified, and start with the talent from Annecy and Kentucky.'

'You will favor them?' Lilou said.

'Damn straight. And you can say so on the website if you want to.'

She nodded. 'We have also been getting pictures from people who live near bitcoin mines; one even has a video with audio so you can hear what it sounds like.'

She put them up on the biggest monitor, and we all huddled close.

I had expected terrible things in the pictures we got. Instead we got photograph after photograph of beauty in the midst of power plants and bitcoin mines. We decided to make it a regular feature on the website.

We made our selections. Two horses. One grazing, one rolling in the grass in a paddock near a dirt road in the woods in eastern Kentucky, a rectangular grid of power lines over their head. The actual mines. One an ugly hellscape, row after row of shipment containers, another in a small rural area of Kentucky, a line of brown and white sheds, a security guard sat out front on a short stone wall, sharing his lunch with a squirrel. He would constitute the whole staff. Bitcoin mines did not bring jobs. You did not need much staff for storing hundreds of high-powered computers and the fans there to keep them cool.

Next up – a woman standing beneath a grassy slope in front of her small white one-story house, crisscrossed overhead by a massive snarl of electrical wires, rows of stubby cut down trees beneath the wires. She held the hand of an eighteen-month-old child who had the stiff uneasy stride of a toddler learning to walk.

'These are beautiful to me,' Lilou said. 'This resilience and grace with hell in the middle. But this next one haunts me. Regardez.'

A video of a two-lane road, school bus stopped to allow a gaggle of children loose. Trees on either side of the road, all of them losing their leaves at the wrong time of the year. You could not see the bitcoin mine, but you could hear it. The loud metallic whine of heavy-duty computers and the fans running to cool them. The noise goes on twenty-four hours a day without end, a soundtrack from hell.

Leo looked up and whined.

'I would go insane,' Lyam said in a whisper.

I stroked Leo's head. 'Let's put it on the Billionaire Blowback page. This is not just about what billionaires do. It's about people living with the consequences. We need to see them too. How this plays out for regular people.'

'So then, Junie, should we post pictures from our office here in VIE, continuing to do our work?' Lilou asked.

'Take a vote. All in favor?'

Unanimous.

'We will be famous,' Matis said.

Lyam threw an Oreo cookie at him. 'We already are. When I go to the Irish bar someone always buys me a Guinness. I am learning to like Guinness. I think it is good for the health.'

'Definitely better than getting shot.' Matis threw the cookie back.

I smiled. My mare Empress had loved a bucket half filled with Guinness and peppermints. Some horse trainers swear by it. She had also liked Cheetos. Flakes of orange on her soft brown muzzle.

'One last thing.' I put my personal invitation flier on Lilou's desk. She glanced at it and passed it around. 'It was delivered to me on my way into the office this morning, by a man in Venetian costume.'

'They are watching you?' Lilou said.

'Worst case, they are watching all of us. Anyone else been approached?'

They had gone quiet. Stunned. There were still bullet holes in the office.

'OK. Keep an eye out. We need to cover this, and put it up on the website.'

Lyam stood up and began pacing around the office. 'But, Junie, that is doing exactly what they want us to do.'

'It's happening, it's real, we can't ignore it. Get a picture of the bouquet, the personal invitation to me, and then we must write this up. We'll report what is happening in this town, how the Vipers are hijacking the carnival for their own ends, how tragedy tourism is seeping into what has been a beautiful thing. We're caught in the middle, right? Between the Vipers and the billionaires, your average person is always caught in the middle like this.'

'Who will write this?' Lilou said. 'Analise, we cannot contact her, she is not on email or WhatsApp – they have her held down tight.'

'I can do it.' Matis spoke so softly, I had to lean close to hear.

'He writes poetry,' Lyam said. 'We need a journalist for this.'

Matis was watching me with soft, worried eyes.

I gave him a nod. 'Poetry is voice. Voice is what we need.'

TWENTY-ONE

It began quietly, the Venetian Carnival, late on a Friday afternoon. Horns honking, shouts, the carousel lit up and spinning. The tourists, most of them French, had been arriving in town since early afternoon. Gathering around the lake, families walking beside the canals, as darkness softly fell.

No debauchery here in Annecy, though Les Vipères Emeraudes would soon change that. The carnival, widely anticipated every year, had the dreamy quality of a dance. The beauty of the players in masks and costumes, silent but engaged. They would pose for you, bow to you, bend down to charm your toddler, who would gaze up at them in thrall.

It began not so long ago, in 1996. Annecy became a sister city to Vicenza, 100 kilometers away in Italy. The Association Rencontres Italie Annecy was formed, one thing led to another thing, and the Venetian Carnival d'Annecy was born.

It began as a three-day entertainment, a presentation podium, animation that sprang to life with a parade that morphed to an ongoing stroll through the city. People made or bought their own costumes, and Venetian masks, mysterious, and intriguing, were the jewels of the costumes. Men in the bauta – black cape, black tricorn, a white mask that covered the face. Women often wore the wolf – a half mask in black velvet or satin. The gnaga cat mask was an ongoing favorite, and the carnival was a luxurious flow of color, imagination, and mystique.

Events would kick off tonight with the Nocturnal Wandering of the Masks. From six o'clock to eight o'clock the carnival players would wind through the pedestrian streets of Old Town, mysterious, beautiful, ever silent.

The mask code of conduct has one inviolable rule – all participants must remain silent. Three days with over five hundred masked Annecy Venetians, silent and mysterious, moving like ghosts through the twisting alleys, the Jardins de l'Europe, Le Pâquier park.

Later, at midnight, Les Vipères Emeraudes would strike. The carnival would go from dreamy elegance and refinement to hardcore horror. They would thrill, they would shock, they would infuriate. They would break the code of silence and they would not be stopped.

It was getting chilly, with the rain and the dusk fading to dark. I ducked back into the kitchen, but Leo would not come in. From the open balcony door, I heard more horns honking, people talking in murmurs on the streets. A bus, several cars, the bark of a dog.

It was hot in the apartment and the cool air felt good. I wondered when Philippe would come home. He was late yet again.

Leo huffed then barked, alerting me. Yet another sighting, another Viper Marquis in black. Looking up at the balcony, staring intently at me. He removed the hat and made a deep bow. In the old days, the costumes gave anonymity, and people from different social classes could meet. Perfect for clandestine lovers, assassins and spies.

He settled the hat back on his hand, put a finger to his lips, then turned, slipping away into the dark. And the point had been made. Les Vipères Emeraudes were watching. I would be expected at midnight tonight on the Pont des Amours, I would be under their protection, and possibly under their thumb.

VIE would say knowledge is power. For Les Vipères Emeraudes, power was knowing what you want . . . and taking it.

Pageantry and death awaited.

I no longer felt protected. I felt stalked.

TWENTY-TWO

Philippe came home late, when it was fully dark. The rain had stopped but the streets glistened in the headlights of the cars. I heard him running lightly up the steps, and he bustled in the door with bags.

'Hello, my beautiful wife, did you miss me?'

'Oh, have you been gone? I thought this place seemed quieter than usual.'

He gave me a kiss. 'I have brought something for Leo. And for you. Come and see.'

He pulled open a package, removing the plastic, and unfolding a magnificent service dog vest. 'He has such a barrel chest, this one, and he is tall like a wolf. I got him an extra large – let me see if it fits.'

Philippe gave Leo a minute to sniff the vest.

A OneTigris tactical dog harness. Full metal black buckles, hook and loop panels. It looked easy to put on and impressive. Strength tested, military grade, durable, and lightly padded for comfort. Long length, not quite loose fit, zero hindrance. Y shape of buckles across his chest for his safety and comfort and no restriction of shoulder and forearm. Three D-rings for every possible leash attachment.

Philippe held up the vest, giving Leo time to give it another once-over sniff, then buckled him in and adjusted the straps. Black vest, red trim. Two arched fabric handles, one at the front and one at the back. I could lift his hind end up the steps if his psoas muscle was bothering him again.

'Look here, Junie, I have ordered patches for the sides. See this?'

We sorted them, made our choices and stuck them to the Velcro. Leo looked like he was ready for battle. He also looked like a billboard. Half of them in English, the other half in French.

DO NOT PET.
HEARING ASSISTANCE DOG.
MAMA SAYS I'M SPECIAL.
SERVICE DOG DO NOT TOUCH.
BEST FRIEND. HOOMAN PROTECTOR.

DO NOT SEPARATE DOG FROM HANDLER.
The vest went from his shoulders to his withers and wrapped around his belly.
'Leo!' I shrieked. 'You are gorgeous.'
He gave me a doggie smile.
'Handsome boy,' Philippe said, petting him backwards along the head like he always did. Leo pranced around the room, going from me to Philippe with a serious case of the zoomies.
'And for you, madame.' Philippe opened another bag.
A photographer's vest, olive green, with six pockets, four that buttoned tight. 'For your keys, and your wallet, and the plastic bags, and the treats, and the clicker, and the lipstick . . . and all of this hands-free. Come, put this on.'
Philippe held it out. Sleeveless, it settled softly over my shoulders, loose, comfortable, nipped in at the waist and the most brilliant bit of clothing I have ever owned. Philippe smiled down at me. 'You see, madame, I think the little vest Leo has been wearing is not enough. Now that we announce to the world that Leo is your assistance dog, they will give you space, and you will no longer be overtaken by bikes and scooters and people moving very fast. I worry that someone will make you fall. You are very vulnerable with that ankle. When people see that Leo is a service dog, they will be kinder, and they will give you space. And tonight, you will need it. It is a carnival on steroids this year. There are fliers everywhere. The Vipers will put on a show, and there will be a massive crowd. You have seen them – the players? They are already in the streets for the wandering. This way we keep you safe.'
I threw my arms around Philippe and gave him kisses, and Leo ran circles around us. Philippe stood at the balcony door and took my hand. It was cool and windy and the darkness was gentle, with streetlights and headlights, and the carousel across the street in Le Pâquier park lit up and spinning. Horns were honking and people were beginning to gather in the street. I saw women in sweeping, full, floor-length skirts, white masks, and hats. Men in boots, tight breeches, scarves, hats, regimental jackets.
Le Carnaval Vénitien had begun.

TWENTY-THREE

I felt like I was walking in a dream, holding Philippe's hand very tight as he pressed close to my right side.

It was forty-seven degrees outside, overcast. Rain was predicted and there had been a lot of it, overflowing some of the canals.

The crowd of tourists was growing thicker on the pedestrian-only Old Town city streets. The carnival players had long finished their nocturnal walk, but they were still out and you could feel the frisson of excitement wherever they went. A ripple of energy in the crowds, heads turning, murmurs of excitement.

Men and women in Venetian costume, always masked. Glorious wigs and headdresses, beautiful dresses, men in regimentals, in jackets and waistcoats, breeches cuffed at the knee, and glorious plumed, feathered hats. Gliding slowly through the crowd, happy to stop for pictures, to spin slowly and turn, to softly touch the shoulders of the little ones who gazed up at them in awe. They were there for the people, the city, the fun. Like Disneyland and Micky Mouse, but low key, elegant. Gentle grace and courtesy. A thrilling presence. The tourists and the locals were content just to watch them, smiling, waving. The Venetians, masked and silent, would hold a finger to their mouth, and stay silent, eyes glinting behind the masks. They were happy to pose for pictures, bow and incline their head. Keeping just a bit of distance, and silent, always.

Tonight, the media presence was stronger than usual and for all the wrong reasons. Local, regional, national, international. And the crowd was moving in the same direction. Toward the Pont des Amours.

Leo, leashed to my waist, was on my left, matching his doggie steps to mine, very proud in his new vest. I smiled up at Philippe, but he was looking ahead and to one side, watchful and tense. Worried. He had told me more than once to stay close, though I was in no shape to wander away.

It was cold out and I could see my breath in the air.

Half an hour before midnight the crowds were heavy and thick. News vans, cameras, microphones. People live-streaming on their phones, influencers stopping in the middle of the street to take selfies against the backdrop of the crowd.

The water had risen over the canal, and flowed onto the walkway to the bridge, which was lit from above and below by red, white, and blue lights. The trees were bare and silvery in the glow of the streetlamps. The green metal railing of the bridge stretched over the canal in a gentle arch.

A man in blue brocade and buckled black shoes appeared at Philippe's shoulder. He bowed to me and motioned us forward. A Viper. They had been on the lookout. They would make sure I had a place on the bridge to watch.

There were citizen reporters working freelance for VIE embedded in the crowd, and all of the locals who live on the internet would also be free to make reports to VIE. It would all be up and on the website in time for morning coffee.

Philippe put an arm tight around me, it was slippery going up the incline of the walkway to the bridge. The man in blue brocade reached out to help me, but pulled back when Leo gave him a warning bark. *Do not touch my Mama.*

I was cold. Shivering in a gust of wind that blew my hair over my face.

The closeness of the crowd made me nervous, but Philippe was right. Leo's new vest made a difference, even in a crowd this energetic, this tight, and people gave us a wide berth and a smile. Les Vipères Emeraudes in Venetian dress surged out of the crowd and formed a buffer around us, a man in blue, a woman in white and gold, another woman in lavender and red, and two other men. They stopped, and the woman in lavender and red nodded her head at me. Who was a Viper and who was simply a costumed Venetian became hard to fathom, there were so many of them, masked, silent, flowing gracefully through the crowd. Disguise, costumes, and silence so you cannot recognize a voice. The thrill of anonymity.

Philippe turned to face me, and pulled me close. 'You know the legend, madame?'

'You mean the emerald of death and the Vipers?'

'Non, madame. I mean this.' He leaned close, and kissed me softly, then pulled me tight and kissed me hard. 'You know what this means when lovers kiss like this on the Pont des Amours?'

'Our love is always and forever.'

'Oui, madame. *As it always has been.*'

And just for an instant he was Olivier come back to me.

I heard sirens. Police, in armbands, and in uniform, were thick on the ground, and tonight they were armed and in vests. Expecting trouble.

It was scary. It was exciting. But I felt an increasing sense of dread, thinking of all the ways that this could get out of hand. Maybe it already had. I could not control Les Vipères. I could barely keep them from controlling me.

But I would not be anywhere else in the world.

It began with the beat of a drum. A funeral cadence. The crowd, breathless, expectant, made way and Philippe tightened his grip on my hand. Three women and three men, carrying tall taper candles, hidden behind their masks and the strange and enthralling beauty of their Venetian costumes. They moved with the measured choreography of a death march to the beat of the drum. One of the men held a square wooden box. He was dressed in the flowy black cloak of the Bauta da Uomo – black tricorn hat, white mask that completely covered his face, and neck. Such a mask would also disguise the voice. His hair was jet back, falling slightly over the collar of his cape which flared out behind him as he walked.

He placed the box in the middle of the bridge. The candles were placed around the box, one by one, and in the flickering light you could see the ornate image of a green serpent with a large emerald in its mouth along every side of the box.

The man in the cape faced the crowd and read from a thick parchment. His voice was loud. Deep. Resonant.

Philippe muttered softly next to me, translating every word so I was sure to understand.

'My friends and citizens of Annecy. I speak to all of us who have rage in their hearts to see the blood of innocent young Annéciens splattered on the streets. Journalists of VIE, living in this city, massacred by a death squad sent by the billionaire Sullivan Carr. Killed because they dared to criticize a bitcoin mine built by the billionaire Sullivan Carr, who had the audacity to locate this mine on the Glières plateau – where our own resistance fighters fought against the Nazi occupation. This nightmare must end.'

The man looked up from the paper and out to the crowd. 'Ses péchés sont les suivants.'

Philippe grimaced as he said the words. 'His sins are as follows.'

Proclaimed in a loud voice and in detail by the man in the black cape were the rest of Carr's sins.

Financial support of a torturers' lobby, sending security forces to torture and kill those who fought for the rights of Guatemala's indigenous population. Making illegal corporate payments to right-wing militia forces in Colombia. Financing armed conflicts in Africa. Business holdings based on price gouging pharmaceuticals.

Eighty percent of his portfolio invested in fossil fuels and climate destruction that killed 1.3 million people due to extreme heat every year.

His annual attendance at the World Economic Forum in Davos, Switzerland, where politicians, billionaires, and business leaders came together to 'improve the state of the world' while they were in reality only improving 'the state of their own interests' – fighting minimum wage increases, restricting unions, and rolling back child-labor laws. Five billion people had become poorer while the world's five richest men more than doubled their fortunes – at the rate of fourteen million dollars per hour.

This would come to an end.

One billionaire at a time.

The man in the cape paused, looking out at the crowd that seemed stunned and in shock. There were murmurs.

He gave them time, then held up a white gloved hand, and the crowd went silent.

He paused, looked out at the crowd, raising his voice.

'Le jugement est prononcé. La sentence est la mort.'

Judgment is pronounced. The sentence is death.

Sullivan Carr had been sent the glittering emerald of death from Les Vipères Emeraudes. He would die by the bite of a poisonous snake.

The Marquis opened the box to reveal the head of a mannequin with gouged-out eyes, teardrops of blood, and a picture of Carr pinned to one side with a small but lethal knife.

There were words in red painted across the mannequin's face.

La Terre nourricière riposte. Mother Earth strikes back.

A woman screamed, and waves of murmurs went through the crowd. The click of cameras and the voice of a reporter were a backdrop as the crowd became a mob. The police pushed forward, shouting commands, drowned out as mob mentality took over and the crowd surged toward the box with the mannequin head. Philippe grabbed me and steered me toward the other side of the bridge – a nightmare of people pushing hard, Leo barking wildly and Philippe pulling me along, moving quickly, too quickly. I could not go so fast; it was impossible with my ankle so swollen and weak, and I was going to fall.

And then he came, La Puce, and three other men, and they circled us and escorted us off the bridge. There were sirens and lights, and I held tight to Leo and Philippe. I stopped once, just for a moment, looking over my shoulder.

The box and the head had been torn to pieces, and the six Vipers were exiting to the beat of the drum, the men and women smiling beneath their masks, as they melted into the crowd and the shadows. The tapers had been left behind, candles flickering in the light.

Sullivan Carr had been judged and condemned.

By the time Daddy Sullivan Carr was having his next morning coffee, this would be up on VIE for the whole world to see, and Carr was really going to lose his shit. But what could he do – send more assassins?

TWENTY-FOUR

There are many ways a town like Annecy could react. All of it covered by VIE, and the number of people accessing our website was astronomical. Hits in the millions. But no word from Analise.

There was immediate blowback to the Vipers, a horror of the violence. Of hijacking the Venetian Carnival, their violent threats, and political ends. What had they done with Analise? Why did they not return her? What right did they have? She needed to go home to her husband, their cows and their farm.

But there was also fury. Over the violent attack on VIE, and a bitcoin mine at a beautiful sacred spot.

In three days, the mine was shut down by decree from the prime minister.

The Bigfoot sightings stepped up, and a man in a Bigfoot costume began regularly showing up at VIE to deliver baguettes.

The Vipers had not created sympathy, but they had created fear.

Exactly their intent.

And it was my job to report this on VIE.

Exactly their intent.

And I had a feeling I would be seeing Le Sorcier again very soon.

TWENTY-FIVE

After the night on the bridge, Philippe worked longer and longer hours, the city got used to seeing Vipers on the streets in Venetian costume on a daily basis, and donations and subscriptions were skyrocketing at VIE. Submissions were pouring in, the staff were working around the clock, and I was having no luck finding a new place for us to rent.

Tonight, Philippe had come home late and hungry. I had made a pot of chili and a pan of cornbread, perfect for the frosty weather. Leo loved cornbread and walking in the cold, and he was sleeping contentedly on the floor next to my feet while I played my guitar. Philippe had been quiet at dinner, and I watched him from across the room.

God, how I loved him. Sitting hunched over the chessboard, focused, shirt untucked, sleeves rolled up, shoes off, soft, worn jeans. He was frowning at the chessboard, and I was aware that my focus on my guitar had been half on the music and half on my husband, whose hair was mussed, his face oddly grim.

He had not moved any of the chess pieces, but instead had been making notations on paper. Chess moves, a hieroglyphic I didn't understand. I liked the presence of those scraps of paper, stacked on the coffee table, the table by the side of the bed, the kitchen table. Part of the background of my life. The steady and comforting flow of Philippe's presence.

He reached for a knight, picked it up, then set it sideways on the board, hand hovering.

'No,' he said, deep and angry, something between a growl and a lament, followed by a backhanded sweep, sending all of the pieces to fall to their death on the chessboard.

'Game not going well?'

The look he gave me was full of fury, but I did not take it personally. I was impressed by his intensity, and for my husband and chess it was always this way.

A page of notations fluttered to the ground, and I picked it up. I saw my name, Analise, Madame Reynard, and then Vipers, La

Puce. All trailing off to letter and number sets that looked like code. And then *midwife* with a question mark.

'This isn't chess,' I said. Leo jumped up on the couch and curled up beside me.

Philippe leaned forward, looked at me, frowning, making up his mind.

For once in my life, I was patient. He was deciding how much and what to tell. If I said the wrong thing, that would shut him down.

Philippe gave me a hard look. I knew he was angry but not at me.

'We need to talk. There are things I must tell you.'

'Ah, yes, those things you were going to tell me that might get me killed.'

It made him laugh, even though he absolutely did not want to.

'Or keep you alive.' He frowned. 'It is Madame Reynard.'

'Oh God, not her again.'

'She is unhappy that you would not talk to her. She thought that you would be useful, and could be controlled.'

'Why would she think that?'

He gave me a half smile. 'Because she does not know you as I do.'

'She has always been very snarky about VIE. Called our launch a slow, stodgy rollout. Said we were only used by academics, pundits, climate change think tanks, and children writing science reports. That we would never have much of a following because regular people did not want to read depressing statistics and examples of rich people destroying the world, though she admitted we have a strong following of viewers who cannot resist the first-hand accounts of weather disasters. She thinks the personal videos and selfies people take while their homes and those of their neighbors are being destroyed are addictive.' I sighed. 'Everything she said was depressingly true. Until Analise.'

He nodded. 'Exactement. But the damage was done before Analise joined VIE. And then it was too late.'

'What damage? What are you talking about? People love Analise, they love her podcast. *Billionaires Behaving Badly* gets more and more viewers. She is funny, she takes the mystique out of the wealthy, she makes people laugh, and she ends the podcast with news of communities making progress so people don't feel so hopeless. She gives them agency. She covers a lot of the good stuff – the first standards for clean hydrogen, adopted by Colorado. The Tulalip Tribes and the farmers in Washington state . . .'

He was not listening.

'Philippe. VIE is a success. We had three million hits after Analise did her first *Podcast in Captivity*, and after what happened on the Pont des Amours . . . it jumped to eighteen million, Philippe. *Eighteen million.*'

'Yes, madame, and that is the problem.'

'Why? Aren't we on the same side as Reynard for once? Her NGO is about climate change solutions; she surely wanted that bitcoin mine construction shut down.'

'But only on her terms, and right now Sullivan Carr is running scared and that makes him dangerous. To her and to you. She is the one who convinced Sullivan Carr to open the mine here in the first place.'

'What the hell?'

'Junie—'

I held a hand up. I needed to think. And then I saw it. 'Because it was so outrageous to put a bitcoin mine on the Glières plateau, she knew that it would not only never happen, it would kick some legislative butt to get the laws she wants in place. Since France has a hard-on for crypto.'

'That is just part of it.'

'No, no, Philippe, this is *great* news. The PM has shut the bitcoin mine down. Carr will be furious with *her* and not *me*. He will send his assassins after Madame Reynard instead.'

Philippe shook his head. 'That is not how it's going to work.'

'But why not?'

'She assured him she could stop the publicity, stop VIE, anytime she wanted.'

'Why the hell did she think she could do that?'

'That is the problem. She can't. You won't even talk to her. Reynard had Carr agree to put a great deal of money into climate change initiatives, which he paid, because she assured him you were *in* on the deal.'

'That bitch.'

'She told him that you would back off as soon as the money changed hands, because it would help accomplish climate change goals. Then, not only did you not back off, you set up this podcast,

he is the butt of jokes with the Bigfoot memes, and then . . . he got the death sentence from the Vipers. The emerald. He was furious, he thought he was playing along, and that you—
'That I fucked him over. That's the only part of this I like.'
'And he told her that if she could not control you, he would.'
'And she didn't warn me?'
'It suited her for him to go after you. It's win-win for her. It made him look worse, and that is exactly what she wanted. She has his money, he has been discredited, the bitcoin mine will never happen, the laws are moving forward, and now the Vipers will take him down so he will not be a problem for her in the future.'
'And half of my staff is dead. So, she has *everything* she wants, including Carr going after me. Because she hates me. You can't tell me this isn't personal, Philippe.'
'Of course it is personal, Junie. She has said so.'
I looked up. 'What did she actually say?'
'Nothing to me; she would know better. But to La Puce. She told him you are an amateur, and VIE was a wildcard. Run by a woman from the American South who did not know her place. I think what makes her dislike you so much is that you do not care about what anybody thinks about you; you are not interested in money under the table, or quid-pro-quo agreements, even if it is for the greater good—'
'The greater good according to Madame Reynard.'
'Yes. But she is right, you care for nothing. Except your dog and your guitar.'
'And you.'
'And I am number one?'
'Right after Leo.'
He sighed. 'I can live with that.'
'OK, Philippe. Know this. I am going to prove it. That she was making deals with Sullivan Carr. And when I do, I'm going to expose her on VIE.'
'Commendable, madame, but very hard to do, and first you must stay alive. And also, there is more for you to know. Reynard is getting blowback.'
'Jesus, get on with it, Philippe, I'd like to know everything before I die.'
'Now that the Vipers are into this, a lot of other very wealthy and influential billionaires are terrified that they too may be featured

on *Billionaires Behaving Badly* and come to the attention of Les Vipères Emeraudes. They do not want to get the emerald and be sentenced to death by snake bite on the Pont des Amours. They are not used to any kind of consequence. All hell is breaking loose and she is in the thick of it.'

'Good.'

'It makes her dangerous to you.'

'Did . . . it was Carr that sent the death squad. Right?'

Philippe gave me a look. 'In truth, Junie, it is looking like they were sent by—'

'Fucking Madame Reynard?'

'I do not yet have definitive proof. I am working on this with Capitaine Babineaux, and she is smart, that one. Reynard knows she can make deals with the Vipers and she thinks eventually she can get them into a working relationship. But she cannot get you.'

I stared at him. 'You know, don't you, Philippe? You know who the Vipers are.'

'When the bitcoin mine started going up, I was assigned by my judge, and there are others of influence behind him, to find out who the Vipers are and how Carr got approval for the mine – which made no sense even—'

'Even with the hard-on France has for crypto.'

'As you say.'

'Well, fuck, Philippe. You're in more danger than I am. Who are they?'

'The wealth managers. Who work for and with the billionaires.'

'*Not possible*. They are like slaves to their wealthy clients. Taking care of every single thing in their lives.'

'And in charge of their money, madame. Which they are moving into dynasty trusts, which means the billionaires have plenty of money but less and less control. Not all of them, of course. Some will not agree to this. The Vipers are a small, close group of very high-powered wealth managers and between them they control forty percent of the billionaires, including at least five of the richest billionaires in the world. Consider, madame. They manage the money, the investments, the businesses, the wives, the children, the mistresses, the wills, the trusts . . . everything. They know every last secret these rich families have, and they are trusted with every detail. They are consulted by governments on how to make the laws to bring the rich investments into their countries, and they have rigged the system so that the very rich are citizens of nowhere and accountable to no one. Whichever way the politics go, they will make money. And gain power. Their clients pay no taxes, and they move through the world like global pirates, citizens of wherever it suits them.'

'So, it is not fascism to worry about but feudalism. I have thought that for a while. And what, they're having regrets? Changing their minds?'

'Believe it. They know that they can get fired if they do not follow every last whim of their employers, and yet they also know every secret, and the dynamic between them has always been about trust, suspicion, and fear. They need each other, and they look over their shoulders, both the billionaires and the managers, and the managers can get fired on a whim. And billionaires have many whims. These wealth managers are not stupid. They see the hurricanes, the floods, and the glaciers melting, and they know that no one has the power to make much of a difference, because they are the ones who set it up, so the billionaires are never accountable; they have themselves written most of international financial law. If this is to be turned around, there is no one in a position to do that except themselves.

'They have children and grandchildren and a stake in the world, and they think it is naive and arrogant and maybe not very smart to rely on underground bunkers in Hawaii while the earth is literally on fire.'

'Oh God, it's like a James Bond movie. They are trying to save the world from evil billionaires bent on the destruction of the earth? Because I have been thinking that I'm the only one who noticed that.'

He nodded. 'They use the Vipers to make their billionaires run scared, and advise them to get out of fossil fuels and bitcoin mines and keep a low profile, and it is already starting to work. So far, they are able to convince them to do everything but let go of the corporate jets.'

'Just the jets would make a hell of a difference. Are you telling me these wealth managers are running around in Venetian costume, stirring shit up?'

He nodded. 'They would trust no one but themselves with this kind of work.'

'More fun than sitting in the office. But . . . La Puce is a wealth manager?'

'As far as the Vipers know, he is muscle for hire. In fact, we have planted La Puce into the organization.'

'He's a spy? For you? Where did you find him? He is not your average bear.'

'I met him when I was very young and new to the police. He and Le Sorcier were together in the French foreign legion; it is brutal and elite and attracts rootless, lonely and violent men, gives them purpose and esprit de corps, and uses them when France needs brutality. When he joined, he was broke, strong, had a criminal record in various Eastern European countries and wanted French citizenship – for which he applied and got after three years in the legion. Most *don't* get it. He did things that . . . impressed. Le Sorcier was there to impress his American father and piss off his French family. His mother was a part of the wealthy French elite. In fact, his mother and Reynard knew each other well when they were young and in the same school. His mother died when he was quite young. He and La Puce did things, as soldiers together that were . . . dark enough to impress and earn La Puce French citizenship. Things you do not want to know. That makes a strong bond between them . . . But not now. Now they are on opposite sides, and they are as likely to kill each other, or to just go out for a beer.'

'Like marriage.'

Philippe gave me a dark look.

'La Puce told me they had been in the legion together. They were greeting each other like long-lost brothers in the middle of the attack on VIE. It's a bromance.'

I put my hands over my face.

'You are OK, Junie?'

'I can't get the images out of my head. When I close my eyes, they . . . just come.'

'I know how this is, but in time it will fade. And I am sorry, but you are alive because of La Puce. He is a very good spy, and he tells us that right now things are starting to move and change. The wealth managers are keeping their wealthy clients happy with their mistresses and various children, legitimate and illegitimate, and lovers hidden from their family, and families within families, and their car collections, and their art. They are advising their clients to go against their short-term interests in order to reverse climate change policy. This is very doable since they are personally responsible for so much of the climate emissions. So yes, they are trying to save the world.'

'Or they are trying to save their ass.'

'They are hardcore, Junie, and without mercy. They hold the reins of empires, you understand? Thanks to them, their clients have the world by the throat. And they want to break that hold.'

'So *they'll* have the world by the throat instead.'

He nodded. 'They will kill you without a second thought if it suits them. You are nothing but a cost analysis to them. If you publish this on VIE right now, both of us are dead. The time may come for that, but it is not now.'

'You are everything to me, Philippe. I won't put it up if it gets you killed, and practically speaking I can't put it up until I can prove it. Who else knows about this?'

'There are a few. My judge and the ones he works with. You, me, and—'

'Madame Reynard. She wants the same thing. To control the billionaires because now it is their turn to be the puppets.'

'You see the stakes here, Junie. Right now, the Vipers find you useful, but Madame Reynard wants you out of the way. Not to mention Sullivan Carr, who is—'

'Losing his shit. Yes. But Leo loves me.'

'As do I. Have I made you more afraid, madame?'

'Honestly? This is fucking awesome, Philippe. A way to control the billionaires and I'm a part of that? I'm thrilled.'

TWENTY-SIX

Another podcast was posted on VIE at midnight the next night. Philippe was out for a 'late-night walk' without Leo, which meant he had someone to meet. Leo stretched out beside me on the couch and chewed on his stuffed llama while I listened.

'*Podcast in Captivity*, episode two.

'Breaking news: In the United States of America, a protestor playing a cello in a city park to protest the Citibank funding of fossil fuels was arrested. A video of this has been posted on the VIE website, so don't take my word for it; go and look.

'This is Analise Morel, reporting to you from hell, where I have somehow lost track of the days I have been in captivity.

'I am being held against my will by Les Vipères Emeraudes, who say they are keeping me safe.

'The truth is that they *did* save my life when the Sullivan Carr death squad gunned down my coworkers and friends at VIE . . .'

I winced. Tried not to think of the ever-growing tally of lawsuits due to Sullivan Carr.

'It *is* true that they guided me through the blood on the floor, and away. Only to keep me in what they call a secure and safe location. But this is a jail, no matter how kindly they bring me food, and give me a comfortable place to sleep. I am seven months pregnant; I need to see my midwife, I want my husband, and I want to go to the barn and see my horse. I have podcasts to do, and a nursery to set up. Stealing my freedom, and using me to put their name in the news, is nothing short of evil; it is a show of power to keep us all in our place.

'I want to go home.

'But be warned, because this is something that all of us climate activists must always consider. Go to the VIE website and read our new page listing "Media owned by billionaires." The *Boston Globe*, the *Washington Post*, the *Minnesota Star Tribune*, the *Los Angeles Times*. *The Atlantic*, *Fortune*, *Time*. The list gets longer and longer and there will be ongoing updates by VIE. Make no mistake, the ones who will shut us down have the money to send death squads, the power to send the police in to haul us away, and the media to hush it, spin it, and bury it under the opinions of pundits who are told what to say.

'How do we protest, mes amis?

'To play a cello to bring attention seems to me a beautiful way, but if you do that in the United States of America you will be taken to jail. There will always be consequences, but do not use this as an excuse for violence or destruction. That is the way of the Les Vipères Emeraudes, and it comes to this – a pregnant journalist held against her will.

'So, I tell you to find your beautiful ways to protest. Do not commit acts of sabotage; do not hurt the very people and the very Earth you are trying to protect. Be peaceful. Be strong. Be ethical. *Do no harm.* That is the Annécien way; it can be the way of the world.

'But be aware of the dangers. Peaceful protesting brings rage. Wealthy corporations set law-enforcement policy, and there will be blowback. *Because they are afraid of you.* Very afraid. Occupy Wall Street struck terror into their hearts, as did the mouvement des Gilets jaunes – the yellow vest protests in France by the working and middle class, crushed between the rising cost of living, disproportionate taxation, and rising income inequality, particularly in rural areas. Their first online protest had one million signatures. Look to VIE, and send us videos, pictures and reports of brutal shutdowns of peaceful protests wherever you live, wherever you are. Share this with the world.

'Together we will hold them accountable.

'Knowledge is our power. Taking a stand is our power. The more of us that do that, the stronger we are. If we join together on this . . . sheer numbers will take them down. Because they have the money, and they own our governments. Standing together is all that we have, and it is powerful. Send VIE your videos of the small things you and your neighbors do to be stewards of our land, show me your farmers markets, show me the small ways your communities make the world safer.

'Remember always, there are more of us than them.

'To my husband, I say I love you. To my midwife, I hope to see you soon.

'It is a joyous thing, to save our world.

'Till next time, mes amis.'

* * *

Analise, who brought the joy and the outrageous attitude of *Billionaires Behaving Badly*, leavened every single podcast with some kind of connection to the natural world. Videos of a whale breaching in the ocean. A dragonfly immigration. Ducks in a pond. Just to remind us. To give us a sense of community and connection. To make us less lonely in the world. Sometimes I was afraid that Mother Earth was going to get rid of us. And that any progress we made was a form of negotiation.

But tonight, Analise had not done that. And something about this broadcast snagged me. I was thinking hard.

I narrowed it down to two things. *Go home to the barn to see my horse. See my midwife.*

She was telling us how to find her so she could come home. But how all of this connected up, I had no idea. I can't do jigsaw puzzles either.

I needed to talk to Stéphane.

TWENTY-SEVEN

Stéphane called me in the middle of the night. I was not asleep. My ankle was keeping me awake, as was this last broadcast from Analise. A glass of wine to put me to sleep would have been a disaster in the making, as unbalanced as I was. And I needed to think more than I needed to sleep.

Horse. Midwife.

The thing about Analise is she is not the kind of woman you could keep in captivity unless you wanted to go to extremes, and every extreme you went to, I guarantee she would go one better. Stéphane said that was why the two of us got along so well. We were difficult.

This meant that Analise was not even close to being safe.

The Emerald Vipers were walking a tightrope with this. The war for public sympathy was on – billionaire death squads, bitcoin mines and oppression from Daddy Sullivan Carr versus rescue, death threats to the obscenely wealthy, and keeping a journalist in captivity because it suited them to keep her alive. I won't say it was a toss-up, but nobody was looking good, and the city of Annecy was still in shock at being caught in the crossfire. For that matter, so was I.

Philippe had come home, chilled to the bone and exhausted. He and Leo were deep asleep, both of them snoring, and I eased silently out onto the balcony and curled up in a chair with a blanket, tried to find a comfortable position for my ankle, which meant propping it up on an upside-down flowerpot.

The pain killed my appetite, and I was taking too much Advil, which also killed my appetite. I decided to cut the dosage in half. The thing that helped the most was my yoga routine followed up by the Assassin Protocol. I was holding hard to my twice-a-day routine.

Stéphane sounded exhausted. Worried. As he would be.

'Apologies, Junie, but we have to talk.'

'I was getting ready to call you.'

I heard the deep sigh.

'You listened to the latest *Podcast in Captivity* tonight? You heard how my wife signed off?' Stéphane's voice was hard and steeped in stress.

'Barn, midwife, horse. She's giving us a pretty clear message, I just haven't exactly sorted it out.'

'Exactement. But I am her husband and I know what she means. What she wants me to do. Though it does not make a lot of sense.'

'What does she want you to do?'

'Go to the barn and get her horse.'

'And then what? Take the horse to the maternity hospital to see her midwife?'

'My older sister, Eve. She used to be a midwife. But she has the degenerative arthritis, so she does not work much anymore; she and her partner live a way out in the valley. She and Analise have never been close – in truth they do not get along – but I think Analise wants me to take her horse there. I can't figure out why.'

'Have you called your sister?'

'Yes. She does not answer.'

'Is that unusual?'

'Between us? No. We are estranged. She does not like my wife.'

'When is the last time you talked to her?'

He made a rude noise. 'We told her when Analise got pregnant. I tried to call her when Analise was taken by the Vipers, to ask how dangerous such stress was for the pregnancy, but she did not answer or return my call. I thought . . . with everything that happened at VIE, she would call me but . . .'

'But yeah. It's odd. I think you're right; Analise may be there. It's a trail of clues so we follow the crumbs. But it's puzzling. Why move the horse now, Stéphane?'

'We had been planning to take the horse home to our farm; it was becoming too expensive at the boarding place and there were—'

'Barn politics, I know.' Sullivan Carr's son had several horses boarded there. He loves the skiing in Chamonix, and every time billionaires love something, disaster follows. I could not seem to escape the Carrs, even in France.

'She will not think her horse is safe there, with Carr's connection and the bad feeling with Carr and VIE.'

Bad feeling was an odd term for death squads, but I let it pass.

'You also have a horse at this barn? She told me about your mare.'

'Yeah, I had a little Arab mare of my own, and I was bringing her over to board there myself. I had already bought a ticket for a horse transport flight from Kentucky to Geneva, but she . . . It was a bad mosquito season in Kentucky and she got EEE.'

'This is . . .'

'Eastern equine encephalitis. She'd had a vaccination, but she got it anyway. She died before I could bring her over.'

'Very terrible for you – I am sorry. This is good to know, this Carr connection at the barn. I have been up all night catching up on chores and making a plan. I will follow what my wife is telling us. I am the husband; I will go to the barn. They will know me. I will pick up her horse, Cooper, and take him to my sister's place, because she is the only midwife I know, other than the one at the maternity hospital. Maybe Analise got away. Maybe she is hiding there.'

'Yeah, Stéphane, it crossed my mind, but why not just give us a call?'

'This is a puzzle, yes. But I am going. First light tomorrow I head out to the barn. You will come also?'

'I'll be at your place by six.'

TWENTY-EIGHT

It was still dark the next morning when Stéphane and I headed out from his farm. It was thirty miles to the boarding place. He was grim-faced when we got to the two-lane road leading up to the barn, and I knew he was full of memories of Analise riding there. I wanted to tell him she would be safe, she would come home, and after the baby was born, she'd be back up on her horse. But it was not my job to make him feel better with bullshit. It was my job to help get her home.

I knew barns like this. You could not grow up in Kentucky loving horses as I do and not know them. And I had wanted a horse of my own from the age of three.

As beautiful as this place was, it did not come close to the horse farms in Kentucky. For that you had to have deep, rich, green grass that people liked to call blue, and the amount of rainfall to keep it that way. Gentle rolling hills. And the kind of money that thought nothing of the expense of perfectly aligned black board fencing, and horse barns that were the stuff of dreams: A-frame, one-story horse chalets, with wide doors, spires, dormer windows. Stall doors built out of the best mahogany, with brass fittings. On the high-end farms, horses lived in a mahogany palace on grounds that had arched doorways in the barn, fountains and small ponds.

If the horse survived their racing days – and many did not – it was a crapshoot of claiming race sales, slaughterhouses, retirement farms for aging racehorses, or an owner who actually had enough heart to keep them.

As the saying goes, if you want to make a million dollars racing horses, be sure to have three million to invest. It's a hard world for horses and people – monetized by the wealthy and the not so wealthy. And billionaires were not the only ones behaving badly. The horse business was a hard way to make a living, and not-so-bad people found themselves doing not-so-great things to survive.

Things got cold and predatory once the private equity hedge-fund bros put their fat meaty hands around the throat of the horse industry, and nothing was ever the same. Terrible things happen when you monetize living creatures with hard, calculating sociopathy.

Most thoroughbred racehorses these days are bred purely for speed, from a dangerously small gene pool. Bad practices that mean horses breaking down at the track. Sometimes I think horses would be better off if they had never met a human.

I bought my first horse when I had been single, running my elder care accounting business with my brother, living in a little Victorian cottage downtown, and newly in love with a French engineer who was in Kentucky on a temporary job. A life that now seemed a million miles away. Empress got left behind while I spent more and more time in France with Olivier, missing the pleasure of grooming my horse, brushing her while she stood quietly, relaxed only under my hand. Deciding, once we settled in Annecy, to raid my retirement fund, and get her a flight through Geneva.

I should never have left her behind, and it haunted me. We had been doing so well, she and I. Once I had taken her off the circuit and stabled her in a little place I rented on my own, I had worked with her by instinct. Once I figured out that Empress was called The Maserati because she was running from the pain, I had tossed the vicious twisted wire bit, and the German martingale that held her head down. But no matter how gentle I was, and how easy her life, she was still afraid. I'm not sure she ever got over that.

I rode her in a little ring and after a year of walking in circles with me talking to her softly, she began to relax and enjoy our little rides, which were all we needed to be happy. She was too dangerous for me to ride outside of the ring, because she had triggers of past traumas I would never know. Her head came down naturally, and she was calm and happy, and looked forward to being brushed and rinsed on hot afternoons. She was the kind of horse that you needed to talk to. To be honest with. To tell her what is going to happen next, and invite her permission.

But the billionaire's boy, Gatsby Carr, the star son who was the pride and joy of Daddy Carr and wife number two, who always got what he wanted, hadn't given up. Mainly because he couldn't have her. And even more, he could not stand that I did. The offers to buy her came in regularly, but I always knew who was behind it, and I always said no. I promised Empress I would keep her safe forever.

When Olivier and I decided to relocate permanently to France,

I boarded her out until I could get her on a flight from Lexington to Geneva. It was expensive, but it would only be the once.

And I learned the hard way that if you don't own your own barn, keeping your horse safe forever is not an easy thing to do. It was more like sending your child to a British boarding school and saying 'Have fun.' Back then I had been trusting and naive and I'd thought all you had to do was pay the exorbitant board fees. I did not understand the danger of hiring out the care of a horse you love.

There are phases in your life you think will go on forever. They never do.

When I'd got the word that my beautiful mare had died, I was wracked with guilt over leaving her behind, coupled with a wrenching grief, and I was out of the horse business for good.

'You love horses, like my wife?' Stéphane asked as he drove up to the barn.

'Very much.'

'And you are from Kentucky, so your mare was a racehorse?'

I laughed. 'Yes, I am from Kentucky. No, everyone there does not have a racehorse. She wasn't a thoroughbred. She was mostly Arab.'

'And you are sure she died?'

I turned and looked at him. 'Why would you ask me that?'

'I have not told you everything. I know the reason Analise wanted me to go to the barn to get Cooper. There is something you need to see.'

I felt the rush of tears down my cheeks. 'What are you not telling me?'

He parked the truck outside of the barn.

'Junie, you must wipe the tears and not look so . . . stricken. They know me here, and there is not much security at boarding barns, but we must stay low key. You are OK now?'

'Yes, I am OK now.'

'Follow me.'

He took my arm and helped me out of the truck, and we wound our way to the back of the barn. He leaned close and spoke in a very low tone. 'There is a horse here at this barn that belongs to Sullivan Carr's son, Gatsby. A mare who is said to be very nervous. And Cooper, he is calm, and they put the mare in a stall next to his, and she is always turned out with him in the paddock. Analise was looking into this when she . . . when VIE was attacked.'

'And she didn't tell me?'

'She wanted to be sure. But this is a Chestnut Arab mare from Kentucky, and the story goes that Carr had been wanting to buy her for a very long time, though he never rides her. She came to the barn eighteen months ago. Before Analise started working with VIE.'

I froze but he urged me forward, looking over his shoulder. 'Keep walking.'

A teenage girl with muddy boots led her horse to a wash bay. A massive Westphalian, seventeen hands high, and muscular. The perfect breed for dressage. Powerful and easy-going. She smiled at Stéphane like she knew him, and he nodded but kept on walking.

Stéphane waited until we were out of earshot. 'Gatsby's story was that the owner finally sold her to him two years ago, and he has been allowing other riders in the barn to show her. But she is a handful. And they have for her a nickname in the barn. When Analise heard that, she got suspicious. What they say about her is she is very fast and takes off the minute you are on her back. They call her—'

'The Maserati.'

TWENTY-NINE

Empress called to me before I saw her. A soft, deep-throated rumble of welcome, tinged with relief. She knew I was there in the way that horses do when you are bonded, because a horse will love you all of your life.

And I now knew why Analise had wanted us to go to the barn. Empress was in the front-and-hind bell boots horses wore for long-distance transport. There was an empty tube of GastroGard on top of a locker outside her stall.

I looked over my shoulder at Stéphane. 'They're getting her ready for transport. They're taking her out of the barn. There's probably a horse van on the way, right this minute.'

'This is why my wife sent us here first, you think? But how would she know this plan of Gatsby Carr?'

I shrugged and turned away. Spoke softly. 'Empress.'

Her head bobbed up and down and she shuffled her feet, and I went into her stall slowly and softly, smiling and talking to her like I always did.

What a beauty she was.

Her coat sleek and shiny, well fed, robust and rounded, mane braided in thirteen delicate plaits, with one more in the forelock. Standing in her stall, on her way yet again to another barn. Hanging outside her stall on a hook was her bridle – a German martingale, a twisted wire bit. The nightmare she and I had left behind.

It brought a sick feeling to my stomach and a fury that I tried to keep banked down. If you've ever seen a horse with blood on its mouth – this is why.

I grabbed the bridle and tossed it into the trash can across from her stall.

'Pretty girl,' I said softly, not at all assured of my welcome. There is nothing like a mare to hold a grudge. She shied away from my hand, and I gave her time. She made nervous rumbling noises in her throat, then nudged up closer, head butted my shoulder, and talked to me the way that horses do.

'Don't forgive me too soon,' I told her, then looked at Stéphane.
'We need to get her out of here before that van gets here.'
'We take her and we take Cooper, he is here in this next stall.'
'Analise says Cooper is really laid back. If these two are barn mates, take Cooper first, and I'll have Empress right behind you. She'll follow him right into the van.'
'You are OK with your ankle?'
'Her ground manners are good.'
'She can come and live with Cooper, Junie. She will have cows to keep her from being lonely.'
'I would love that, and I'll pay a fair board fee.' It sounded like a dream come true.
'If you leave that bridle in the trash, they will know it is you who took her.'
'Good.' Focus on the horse. Bank down the rage.
Stéphane was kind enough to take in stride that I was crying.
'So, I am thinking that Analise has made us rescue the horses before we find her.'
'And just in time.'
'I wonder how she knew this. And why it was important to get the horses first.'
'Because tomorrow, Empress would have been gone, and the odds of me finding her again would be zero. But how she knew, and why now . . .' I was happy to have Empress but I was very afraid that this would put Analise at more risk. Gatsby was not going to be happy about this and neither was Sullivan Carr. We needed to get Analise out.
'We'll ask her when we find her,' I said.
'You think we will find her?'
'I think she is three steps ahead of us, so yes, I do.'
Analise was in captivity. With plenty of time to think.

THIRTY

I led Empress up the ramp and into Stéphane's trailer. I had never thought I would walk beside this horse again.

'I am not leaving you,' I whispered to her, and she nickered low in her throat.

Stéphane secured her ties with a practiced hand. I had not seen him with animals and I liked his low-key, steady presence. I could see Empress relax under the touch of his large, calloused hands. Empress and Cooper exhaled snorts and throaty murmurs, once they were together in the trailer. Barn mates and paddock pals.

Stéphane gave me a look. 'Analise says they are in love.'

There are those who discourage these deep friendships between horses, a bond that could grow so strong the horses became unhappy and agitated when separated. These issues can be dealt with if you have half a brain. Many people don't.

It was worse than the usual farce, me climbing back into the cab of the trailer, with an ankle that I could not put weight on, an ankle I was afraid of twisting again. I tossed my bag in and grabbed the door handle, then heard Stéphane say *wait* softly.

I got my good foot up on the first step and maneuvered in sideways. He kept one hand on my arm, the other giving me a boost, and I scrambled in, off balance but knowing he would not let me fall.

'Elegant as always,' I muttered.

He bent close. 'Don't look over your shoulder, but clock the guy by the side of the ring when we drive by.'

''Kay,' I said under my breath.

'What is this Kay? You know him?'

'Short for OK.'

'Kay,' he said softly, and I knew he was happy with this tiny treasure of American slang. The French have a weakness for English phrases that are short, pithy, and to the point.

He climbed behind the wheel, fired up the engine, and shifted into gear. It was an old truck. Well-maintained, but noisy.

I glanced into the wide side-view mirror as we passed the ring.

'Ah,' I said.

Stéphane nodded but kept his eyes on the road.

He was damned attractive, this dude I was watching in the mirror, I had to admit. Denim shirt and jeans, and a compact athletic build that he'd had to work for. Deep tan, shoulder-length dark blond hair. He was carrying a saddle that he set upside down and flat on the ground, instead of sideways, propped on one side, the way anyone who had ever seen the inside of the barn would set it.

'He looks like trouble,' I said.

Stéphane nodded. 'I'm glad to be out of that place, and I am thinking that you and I and this truck are exactly the ones he was waiting to see. Whoever this is, he is trying to find my wife.'

'Yeah, no doubt he heard the podcast. And I'm thinking he was supposed to. The good news is, he's on foot.'

'You think he cannot park a car?'

'Oh shit. Yeah, he is watching us and reporting to somebody on a cell phone.'

Stéphane squinted into the sun. 'It is odd how they are out in the open with all of this.'

'I think that's kind of the point.'

THIRTY-ONE

Horse trailers and brakes always made me nervous in heavy traffic and on steep roads. If you go too fast, and get sway in the trailer, you've got a problem on your hands.

'I don't see anyone following us.' I had been watching behind us for the last forty-five minutes.

It was a two-lane road at this point, winding up the side of the mountain, and Stéphane was taking it slow and easy, which meant the horses were not getting slung around. Stéphane was a good driver, but it was a hell of a route for trailering a horse.

He didn't even glance sideways, his eyes on the road. 'If they were following us, we'd know it. That's not what is worrying me. They know where we are going, I think. They could find another route and get there before we do.'

'Well. Your sister's not a secret, is she? She's a midwife. They sure as hell could figure that out. At the barn, he was positioned to see which way we turned.'

'Yes, I thought of that. I went in the direction of home; it would be normal for me to take my wife's horse home to our farm. Just on the chance they might be fooled. Who do you think they are?'

'Assassins. I am beginning to recognize the type. They'll be at your sister's before we are. They'll be waiting.'

He nodded. 'Yes, that is what I have been worrying about. That they will get to my wife.'

'They could have gotten to her without following us.'

'They are rounding all of us up.'

I didn't like the sound of that, but I didn't say it out loud. 'That rifle you've got hanging in the back—'

'Le fusil?'

'Is it loaded?'

'Oui.'

'You a good shot?'

'Si, si.' The road leveled off, and he pulled to one side, reached round behind him for the rifle. 'And you? From Kentucky and the American South, you can shoot? I have a pistol in the glove box.'

I thought back to the last time I had fired a gun. Killing St Priest and Béatrice.

'I can handle it.'

THIRTY-TWO

The next time I saw the handsome assassin from the barn, he was sprawled half in and half out of an expensive rental Range Rover, standard assassin black. His head was canted sideways out of the open door, long hair streaming in soft downward waves, blood still leaking from a bullet hole between his eyes. The car had rolled to an uneventful stop on the side of the road, one foot from a tree, the airbag had not gone off, and the engine was no longer running.

Except for the blood, his hair looked soft and lush. I wondered what kind of assassin shampoo he used.

La Puce was there, wide grin on his face, as he flagged us down. He was rolling a plastic sheet out on the road, and he nodded at me over one shoulder. Tight red flannel shirt that looked worn and soft, tight jeans, and work boots with steel toes, the better to kick your ribs in with.

'Bonjour, Junie.' Just another day on the job. He flipped me a wave. 'Where is Leo?

'Leo is not good with horses. He wants to herd them.'

Stéphane turned the truck engine off and jumped down to the road. 'Salut, Monsieur Cambronne. I am here to rescue my wife. Please give her back to me. I must also check on the welfare of my sister.'

'Ah, bonjour, Stéphane, yes, you are expected. That has all been arranged. Analise and I were hoping you and Junie would come and lead these assassins to me, but they arrive before you do.'

I stopped halfway out of the truck. *They*?

Stéphane grabbed my waist and eased me gently to the pavement, then looked over his shoulder at La Puce. 'You need some help with him?'

'Ah, non.' La Puce dragged the assassin with the great hair on to the plastic, rolled him up deftly like a man who had done this many times in his life, and loaded him into the back section of the Range Rover. I could see that the back was crowded with leather luggage, weapon cases, and the saddle that had been upside down on the road near the barn. La Puce had to shove and fold him in a little.

'I must thank you and Junie for smoking them out.'

'How many more are there?' I asked.

'Two we know of for now, yes, yes. You were the bait, of course; you led them away from Analise and to yourselves. We have this one here but the other has slipped away. No matter, I will find him. He is subpar, the only kind available to billionaires, most of the good ones get hired out by governments, but I underestimated him.'

He shrugged. 'It happens.'

'My wife?' Stéphane said.

'Yes, yes, she is OK. She has been here with your sister and her partner all of this time, safe and sound, and well guarded.'

Stéphane stopped and stared at La Puce. 'And you have been holding my sister hostage as well? All of this time?'

La Puce went still. Spoke kindly. 'Your sister agreed to give Analise safe harbor; this was arranged and paid for. *Generously* paid for.'

'Are you saying my sister agreed not to tell me, even when I called her to tell her what happened to my wife, and told her how worried I was? When I asked her if there was a risk to my wife's pregnancy, with all of this stress? Because I do not believe you. Not even Eve—'

'She agreed to the terms in advance. Safer for everyone that way.' La Puce shrugged. 'I am sorry but there seems to be trouble in your family. Analise said there was animosity with you and your sister, and it was all her fault. But perhaps your sister felt it would be better this way.'

Stéphane rubbed a hand over his face. Took a hard breath, then went very still. 'I want my wife back. That is all that matters to me. And I want her now.'

'Monsieur, there is much you do not understand and much I cannot explain. Please know that I did not want to keep your wife from home like this, but that I had no way around it until today. Then your wife and I, we made this plan. This is the soonest we could get her out. Safety under the gun is not safety. Please remember who it was who got you and Analise out that day when VIE was attacked. I did not know of the plan to take your wife until she was already gone. But they did have good reason, as you see from this one who is still leaking blood, even if you and I do not agree.'

I put a hand on Stéphane's arm. 'Trust him,' I said.

He looked at me hard.

'Trust him.'

La Puce gave me a friendly smile.

Stéphane headed back to the truck. 'You say my wife is at my sister's? I will go up to the house and get her myself.' He glanced back at La Puce. 'She had better be there, and she better be OK.'

'Monsieur, non, your wife, she should be home by now. Your sister is taking her there. To your farm. You sister was actually paid by the Vipers to take your wife to your farm once we cleared up the threat. I am waiting for a call from Analise to confirm she is safe home, which should come at any minute.'

Stéphane's cell phone rang.

'Ah,' La Puce said. 'That will be your wife. She calls you first, of course. Tell her everything is being taken care of.'

'You will please stay right where you are, monsieur, while I talk to my wife.'

Stéphane climbed inside his truck. I could see from his face when he answered the phone that it was Analise. It was a short conversation, but he was a different man when he got out of the truck. Relief and fatigue.

Stéphane studied La Puce. 'My wife says I am not to kill you.'

La Puce gave him a wide smile. 'I am not looking for a fight, Stéphane. I have had one today already, and there will be another, I hope before dark, because I have plans for dinner tonight. And now, monsieur, you must get home to your farm and to your wife. You are to be congratulated for coming so quickly.'

Stéphane frowned. 'Will the Vipers come after her again?'

'No, they were trying to keep her safe; I am their head of security, I know this to be true. I have just one more to kill, for now anyway, and we cannot keep her forever; your wife is very pregnant, and the publicity for the Vipers is turning bad. I will see that you and your wife will be protected. You live at the top of the slope, monsieur, easy to defend. You won't even know I am there.'

'I'll know,' Stéphane said.

La Puce gave him a look. 'You have not clocked me yet. But your sister . . .'

'Quoi?'

'She is family to you, but she is not to be trusted. Get her out of your house.'

It is not possible to drive quickly with a loaded horse trailer. It was a white-knuckle drive home.

THIRTY-THREE

Stéphane's sister Eve was waiting on the porch of his chalet farmhouse when we arrived, parked outside the barn with the horses. Stéphane invited me into the house, but I shook my head and said I'd help Eve get the horses settled in the barn. I would give him time for a private reunion with Analise and then I expected all hell to break loose with Stéphane and his sister.

That was the plan we had made in the car. We would make sure the two of them were never together again. He would talk to Analise and they would decide what we should do next. For now, we would get his sister out of the house.

In truth, it was a challenge just to get myself out of the truck.

Eve watched me hobble to the back of the trailer. She was a looker in her fifties. Dark chestnut hair, very thick, cut shoulder length, generous curves, dark eyes. The definitive limp of a very bad right knee and lines of chronic pain in her face.

'You look in no shape to be leading a horse,' she said. Very French, very blunt, which were often one and the same. I didn't expect to like her, and I didn't. She had an edge to her, an ingrained arrogance, as if everything was going to her private plan and I was just a bit player and of no importance in a world where she was in charge.

In truth she was right. I was not in any shape to lead a horse, but on the other hand, if you never went to a barn when you got hurt, you were not going to be in a barn very much.

'Just let Cooper go first, and my horse will follow.'

She was even better at getting horses off a truck than her brother. She had done a lot more in her life than deliver babies. I would not want to be pregnant and at her mercy. And she was not going to touch my horse.

Empress was white-eyed and picking up her feet, but she was happy to follow Cooper into the barn, and she gentled pretty fast as I spoke to her in low tones. The copeaux de bois – wood shavings as bedding for the horses – were spread generously, which Empress would like. There was fresh cold water in a bucket attached to the wall, and I was delighted to see she and Cooper both had two flakes of fresh Doulière Hay – a top-of-the-line wholesaler of alfalfa hay which was exported all over the world. I looked up, saw the dense, compressed bales were stored in the loft, wrapped to protect them from humidity and dust.

The barn was clean, everything in place, no dark corners of cobwebs and dirt and no rusty tools. Plenty of feed, hay, and shavings.

And the cows. Well fed, glowing with health. Empress rolled her eyes at the cattle grazing outside near the barn. She would have to swallow her outrage in sharing a barn with cows. She was an opinionated Kentucky snob mare, and she did not like cows, goats, or potbellied pigs in a barn or near her paddock.

Stéphane was waving his sister into the house, and I heard Analise call to me. I closed the door to Empress's stall and headed out of the barn.

I would have thought she would be too pregnant to run, but it was unwise to underestimate the energy of a woman like Analise. She looked awkward, her belly huge, long brown hair piled in an outrageous mess on her head, and lines of exhaustion and stress in her face. It was high damn time she was home.

'Junie, *Junie*. I had to come see and know you were safe. I thought that day they had killed you, I heard the shots, and Leo growling, and then yelling and then everything quiet. And they hustled me out, there was not time—'

She took both my hands and kissed my cheeks. She sounded breathless. 'They told me you were OK, but I had to see you for myself.'

'Same here. You can't even know how glad I am to see you.'

She brushed tears out of her eyes, and I glanced over her shoulder. Stéphane was out on the porch with his sister, Eve, watching us, then he gave me a hard nod and put a hand to his sister's back, getting her into the house.

Analise looked exhausted, worried and rumpled in a huge loose flannel maternity shirt, baggy jeans. Her eyes were bright and so green.

'You look beautiful,' I told her. 'I was so worried about you.'

'Yes, I did not want to have my baby in captivity, with my Satan of a sister-in-law, and he will come soon, this baby of mine, we are down to just a few weeks.'

'How is it you look—'

'Well fed?'

'Full of energy. After being held captive for all these days.'

She laughed. 'It is not me but Eve who suffered. I made her life a living hell, I promise you that.'

'Philippe and I have been so worried about you. But I told him you'd be giving them trouble.'

'Ah, your husband, the formidable Philippe, his name came up more than once, these Vipers were quite worried what he would do.'

'Were they? My sweet Philippe?'

'I think you do not know your husband in the way others know him, Junie.'

'What woman does?' I said. But I wondered.

'Ahh, no, look at you standing sideways, they have shot you in the foot. I knew it, I knew—'

'No, no. I just . . . fell.' I did not want to tell her that I had slipped in blood. It was not an image she needed in her head.

She put a hand to her forehead. 'I have been so homesick.'

'Your episodes of *Podcast in Captivity* have been fabulous, Analise. We had over three million hits on the first one, and we have had eighteen million hits since then.'

She smiled at me. 'I know. I was keeping track.'

We looked at each other. So much to say.

She looked over my shoulder, shrieked *'Cooper'* and ran to her horse, who had stuck his head through the little dip and yoke of the half-stall door. Metal, economic, rugged.

'Ah, Cooper, mon chou chou, mon caramel, mon nounours.'

Her darling, her soft caramel, her teddy bear. I sometimes called Empress *Baby Girl*. I was going to have to up my game.

She moved to the next stall, and Empress came to the stall door and stood quietly to be told she was la petite bébou.

'You are so happy to have her back? Oh, no, don't cry, Junie.'

'I don't understand how this happened. What she is doing in France. None of this makes sense to me; it is like a dream.'

'Yes, I will tell you everything. But, Junie, Stéphane is in the kitchen with his bitch of a sister, and you and I must talk fast. I did not escape to her little shitty place in the middle of nowhere. That is the place Les Vipères took me the day VIE was attacked. Eve was paid, and paid well, to keep me there. She is why no one found me. The Vipères chose her to keep me captive because they could be assured that if I had my baby, I would be safe. I know they have saved my life, and my baby and you and Stéphane, but they are arrogant, these decisions are mine, not theirs. And for Eve to go along with this . . . she betrays her brother and she betrays me. And if they knew my sister-in-law . . . Yes, she was a midwife, but she was not a good one, and she did not retire because of arthritis. I have lived in great fear that the baby would come early.

'The police must know that I am safe home now – and also I *must* denounce her; she cannot get away with this. Does maybe your husband know a cop who will believe me? I want someone hard and skeptical, who will not believe her lies. Someone very tough.'

I smiled. Picked up my phone. Reverse dialed because the very cop we needed had called me more than once.

'Who is this you are calling?' Analise asked. 'This is someone you know?'

'Capitaine Babineaux? Yes, I'm afraid I know her well, and she is exactly the one you want.'

Analise waited, eyes closed tight, and looked up when I was done.

'She's on the way,' I told her.

'Right now, she really will come?'

'You couldn't stop her if you tried.'

'Oh, Junie, I am so glad you know this one.'

She grabbed my hands. 'I have missed you, Junie. You make me feel safe in the world. And I will not go back into the house while my sister-in-law is here.'

'We'll let Capitaine Babineaux clean this up. I am so grateful to you for bringing Empress home, but none of this makes sense to me.'

She nodded. Settled carefully on a hay bale, and I had an attack of guilt.

'You know, never mind. Are you cold? Let me get you a blanket and something to eat. I won't let Eve come near you. You should rest.'

'Do not be ridiculous, Junie, I have done nothing *but* rest. I will stay right here until your police person comes. If I have to spend one more second with my sister-in-law, I will take a knife out of the kitchen drawer and stab her in the neck. And there are things you need to know.'

Not the first time I'd heard that in less than a week.

'La Puce, I have to say he becomes a friend to me. I know he is an assassin and very bad but . . . he saved my life. Deux fois.'

'Two times?'

'The first time you were there. The second time? Today. He takes down two more assassins so I can go home.'

'La Puce said you would be safe here. He would be keeping an eye out.'

She nodded. 'He came up with this plan to get me out as soon as it was OK. He was honest with me, and I think that is how I survived. He has a heart, that one. And I think he is not just a Viper. I think he is also working with someone in secret, with the police. But I don't know for sure, and we will not breathe a word of this through VIE. Until the time comes. If it ever does. I will not betray him. You must agree to this, or I will not talk to you about this anymore.'

'You can trust me on this, Analise.'

I had a sudden need to sit down. Analise had the straw bale, so I propped my back to the stall, and eased myself onto the ground, stretching out my leg to get my ankle in a better position. It hurt like hell. As soon as I got home, I would take as many Advil as I wanted. So much for cutting the dose in half.

And of course, I knew who La Puce was working with. This someone secret with the police. Philippe, the man I slept with every night. My husband, almost a stranger, and damn, he was sexy as hell. There was a little part of me that was thrilled. I was trying to wrap my mind around the thought that this was my actual husband. The problem was becoming how to keep him alive.

But God knows, I would keep my mouth shut. I would not betray my husband, or La Puce, not even for VIE.

THIRTY-FOUR

Analise tilted her head to one side, thinking. 'So, to begin. You say having your horse back is a dream, but a good dream, yes? Because there are those who will not like it so much. Evidently, Junie, when Gatsby Carr found out you were moving your horse to Geneva, to keep in the French Alps, he was furious. He grew up skiing with his father in Chamonix, and to think you are there with a horse he wants for himself, having a life he does not think you deserve . . . And now suddenly he and his father have a thing for the French Alps. He wants your horse, and he wants to ride her in France, because if you want it, he wants it to. This is explained to me by La Puce.'

'And how did La Puce know all of this?' But I realized I knew the answer to my question.

'La Puce knows the wealth manager for the Carrs. He is one of Les Vipères Emeraudes. And that is who they are, Junie. These Vipers are all the wealth managers to the billionaires. They run their lives.'

I tried to look surprised.

'It is true, then, she is your Maserati? And I knew it the moment I heard her name from La Puce. La Puce tells me that they have Emerald Vipers watching you, Junie, even when you do not know. He called it "shadow work." He found out about Carr's son Gatsby, and how he stole your horse, because it was told to him by the wealth manager for Sullivan Carr.'

'They said my horse was dead.'

'But you were in Annecy, yes? This barn manager where you boarded your horse, she made a deal with Gatsby Carr. She tells you that your horse is dead, so very sorry, madame, and this pig person is paid off to sell your horse to Gatsby Carr. And he brings The Maserati here, because you are here, to show you he can have whatever he wants. He wants you some day to find this out. He has papers that say you sold her to him. With his money and lawyers, how will you ever get her back unless you do what you have done today?'

'Ah yes. French attorneys. So of course I would have to steal her. Thank you for setting that up.'

She nodded. 'This is OK with you?'

'It's not stealing when the horse belongs to me. '

'Your horse will be safe here with Stéphane; he will not let Carr take her. I think I could shoot him with the rifle we have.'

'Thank you.' I only had conversations like this with Analise.

'And so it happens this way. La Puce is in charge of security, and he says it is time to let me go. He goes straight to the wealth manager of Carr, who is unhappy. Carr is getting such bad publicity, he thinks he will be fired. He is British, this one, from a society family, very old. La Puce says yes, it is time to let me go and this will happen soon. Le Brit, as La Puce calls him, says the sooner the better because Carr is out of hand and has a thing for punishing you, and his son has even stolen your horse. Because that is where it started. Your horse and some love affair Gatsby had—'

'With my brother.'

'Your brother, yes.'

'This is so fucking petty. I moved to France to get away from these people, and here they are, dammit.'

'It is always the way with such people, Junie. These ones, they cannot hear "no." According to La Puce, Carr is one of the worst of the worst for tantrums. Le Brit says Carr wants the horse shipped back to their place in Florida, since they have shut down their mine in the Alps.'

'Florida? In that kind of heat?'

'Yes, your horse will not like that; she is happy here in France with Cooper. And La Puce, he just smiles but he is enraged that they are taking your horse. La Puce, he and I talk together, and come up with a plan to get the horse safe, and the assassins out in the open. And we have to move fast, before they take Empress away.

'So, I let you and Stéphane know what to do, hoping you will figure out what I say in the podcast, and the two of you will handle the horse side of things, while La Puce, he takes care of the rest. La Puce arrives and tells Eve to take me home, and he gives her a packet of euro in cash, and more to come later for what he says is severance pay. So evidently it worked out and these men were not a problem. But I worry a little they will find me here.'

'They won't,' I said.

'You don't think?'

'I don't. La Puce already killed one of them and he says he'll kill the other one tonight, and then will make sure no one comes after you again.'

She nodded. 'It would seem fair for me to kill Eve. Or maybe he could do it?'

'No, truly, the worst thing that can happen to her is Capitaine Babineaux. You'll understand when you meet her.'

'I will not go back into the house while my sister-in-law is here.'

'No, no, don't do that.'

'But Capitaine Babineaux needs to get here soon. I don't want to be forever on this bale of straw.'

But that is where I left her, and she promised to stay where she was. I did not want to be there when Capitaine Babineaux arrived. I gave Empress a kiss goodbye. She headbutted me but did not veer off from her flake of alfalfa, happy to be in a barn with Cooper. She knew she was safe.

THIRTY-FIVE

I pulled over on my way home to call Philippe. He answered immediately.

'Junie, you ignore my texts.'

'I have been out of range. But I have news.'

He listened quietly and without comment as he always did. 'So, there is one more hunting you?'

'La Puce seemed sure he would have him by tonight. If it is a *him*.'

'How far are you from home?'

'I'm close. I thought you'd be happy about Analise. You don't sound happy.'

'I will promise to be happy when you get home safe. Do not leave the house without Leo again. Or me, for that matter.'

'Let's get real, Philippe. This is intimidation. Madame Reynard and billionaire games. Kill me and they lose. They have to make me back down. In a way that makes them look good, because the world is watching now. If they really wanted to kill me, I'd be dead already. You're the one I'm worried about.'

'You are very kind, my Junie. Come home now; I want to see you here safe.'

THIRTY-SIX

The next morning, two men washed up on the shores of Lake Annecy. Neither of them had drowned. Both had died by a bullet to the head, one of them blond with the bullet between his eyes. Both had a note attached to their backs with a knife.

Les assassins seront tués. Assassins will be killed.

The Emerald Vipers made their actions clear in the usual way. A flyer that they handed to people at night in the streets, dressed in Venetian costume. That they hung on streetlamps. That they stacked up outside of doorways. They plastered them to the windows of restaurants.

Sans Pitié pour les Assassins – No Mercy for Assassins

When billionaires send death squads to Annecy to attack our citizens, they will be killed. We regret the time citizen journalist Analise Morel spent in captivity, against her will, but we had word of two death squads very close who were stalking and tracking her down. They have been taken care of, and Analise Morel has been set free.

Our apologies for the inconvenience.

THIRTY-SEVEN

Analise had missed all three of the funerals. These were private burial arrangements where I had been made welcome, Philippe by my side, Stéphane Morel riding with us. Those of us left at VIE felt a strange relief in each other's company, having survived together. All of us staying grouped closely, stunned and in shock.

'This is not your fault,' Philippe would whisper to me afterward, when I could not sleep at night.

VIE had been planning the memorial service, at the request of all three families. To be held once Analise came home safe.

She had taken two days to rest and to go over the details, and under her brilliant guidance, the memorial service we would hold would draw the media, offer the families a bit of grace, honor our dead, would engage and bring hope . . . and work the spin.

I was nervous as hell.

I wore black. Black tights, black ankle boots, a size and a half up to pull over my ankle, still wearing the brace. Black pencil skirt, black sweater, a peacock-blue half jacket with large gold buttons, and a *don't-fuck-with-me* attitude that was palpable.

My lipstick was deep glossy red. Amour.

Philippe took my arm and kept me steady as I limped up the flimsy metal steps to a wide podium we had erected in Le Pâquier park.

'This is so embarrassing, to hobble like this,' I told Philippe.

He shook his head. 'Let them see it. You are alive and that is what matters. You earned it.'

'I fucking slid in blood.'

Getting up the stairs to the stage was the hard part. Now I was up, I would be OK.

I looked out from the stage to the lake on my left, the carousel ahead, and to the right, the canals and the Quai Eustache Chappuis, Le Splendid Hotel on the corner. There were people on the balconies watching.

Philippe stood next to me like a bodyguard, expensive black suit, white shirt, gold cufflinks, wedding band that matched mine. My ankle was unsteady and I held tight to the podium.

I had no script. I knew exactly what I wanted to say. The limits of my French meant I would keep it short.

La Puce had promised to have men keeping watch. Vipers he could trust. It was an uneasy seesaw between The Emerald Vipers and VIE, and the Vipers were all through the crowd, wearing Venetian costume, bowing with charm and grace to photographers. Their pictures would be everywhere by the end of the day. Score one for Les Vipères Emeraudes.

I put both hands on the podium, looking out at the crowd. The families of my staff. Their friends. It looked like the whole of Annecy was there, and the international press was everywhere. Film crews, photographers, microphones, white trucks with their equipment. Possible assorted assassins. Swans in the canals, and dogs on leashes. And the thick presence of the police. Everywhere. Expecting trouble. Under the hard-ass supervision of Capitaine Babineaux.

'Bonjour, mes amis,' I said. Echoes of my voice from the microphone. 'I speak to you on behalf of VIE. Verité, Information, Egalité. An open-source intelligence NGO that brings information to the people and access to all. Information gathered by regular people like you and like me, citizen journalists from everywhere in the world, and on the ground as the events of the world unfold. Sharing information because knowledge is power. Truth to the people without media spin, and without suppression.

'To those who accuse us of taking sides, I say . . . *you bet we do*. We take the side of truth, and we know who to blame. Our world is being destroyed by the wealthy elite who have allegiance to no one – global pirates who will never be satisfied and take what they want. Who think they are safe behind barriers of power, influence and secrecy. And they are bringing the earth to its knees.

'This is your world that is being crushed by billionaires so obsessed by greed they do not care if the world goes up in flames; who think they will be safe in their underground bunkers while the rest of us die. If it is secrecy that keeps them safe, our open-source intelligence will see they are safe no more.

'Billionaire tech-broligarch "Daddy" Sullivan Carr tried to use his power and influence to build the ravenously power-consuming and greenhouse-gas-emitting ecological *carnage* of a bitcoin mine on the Glières plateau. He got shut down, thanks to VIE.

'A death squad was sent to silence VIE.

'But VIE will not back down. The pictures I show you will be graphic. Some of you may prefer to turn away. But we will *not* normalize what happened in the offices of VIE. And we *will* show this to the world.'

This brought cheers, which stopped abruptly when the first picture hit the screen.

The office wall splattered with blood; the glass of the French doors shattered across the floor. Our BILLIONAIRES SUCK banner hanging sideways, marked with bullet holes.

'Today we honor the members of VIE who gave their lives, assassinated right here in this city, for daring to expose the truth.'

The pictures of my staff went up on the screen and I called out their names.

'Louis Romilly, Research, gunned down. Clementine Allard, Visual Analysis, gunned down. Timothée Fornier, Master of Tech, gunned down. Analise Morel, Citizen Journalist, targeted for death, kidnapped, escaped.' There were cheers and shouts when her picture went up.

'VIE cannot be stopped. There are too many of us.' And the pictures and names filled the screen as I called out the names. 'VIE is all of us. VIE is everyone. VIE is Danielle from Queensland, Aya from Syria, Garth from Tennessee, Randy from Wisconsin, Kelli from Michigan, Stephen from Leeds, Geoffrey from Scotland, Sian from Wales, Madisa from South Africa, Dieter from Berlin, Franck of Paris. VIE is everywhere. VIE is you and me.

'And we have news for you that is good. Our efforts to shut down the bitcoin mines all over the world are ongoing and we are getting unexpected help.'

Now came the Bigfoot pictures. Laughter rang out along with cheers for each Bigfoot picture that popped up on the screen. We had new ones to add. Bigfoot mooning the bitcoin mine. With a baguette. Bigfoot walking a dog wearing a vest that said *Billionaires Suck* past the bitcoin mine construction sight, while feeding the dog a baguette. Bigfoot laying a bouquet of flowers and a sack of baguettes to honor the dead in front of the office of VIE. Bigfoot riding the carousel wearing a tee-shirt that said *Billionaires Suck*, while eating a baguette.

'I am sure many of you have been following the *Podcast in Captivity* from Analise Morel, after she survived the carnage of the death squad that attacked VIE.'

The crowd went quiet.

'We are thrilled and relieved to announce that Analise Morel returned home safely forty-eight hours ago, and not only did she consent to be here with us today, we could not keep her away. We invite you to share in our joy and gratitude that she is now safe home, and back to work with VIE. May I introduce award-winning citizen journalist, and VIE podcaster, Analise Morel.'

The applause was deafening as the crowd made way. Analise forged ahead to the podium, heavily pregnant, full of energy and fierce, under the escort of four armed and uniformed police.

I stepped back and pressed close to Philippe. Once Analise was at the microphone, I could breathe again. My part was done.

Philippe gave her a hand as she climbed up the stairs to the stage. She looked out at the audience, serious, steady, and calm.

'Today we begin again at VIE. The blood has been washed away, the memories will not fade, and you will find us at our regular office on the Square de l'Evêché, where I will continue my regular podcast, *Billionaires Behaving Badly*. I know many of you are worried for us, and in truth we are still under threat.'

Another image went up on the screen. Me, with the assassin, which had become caricature and meme.

'Assassins watch our staff. Our own Junie Lagarde has been stalked in the streets of Annecy. But VIE will not back down. I tell you to let go of your daddy's musty, fusty, dusty spy organizations, and welcome you to VIE, where we are the spies of the people, by the people, and for the people. Spies of liberté, égalité, fraternité. We are the spies in plain sight.'

As I looked out into the cheering crowd, Analise grabbed my hand and we raised our arms together as the crowd shouted VIE, VIE, VIE.

A man in a black wool Venetian coat and high boots doffed his hat and bowed to us. La Puce. On the job and watching.

The theme song of the *Billionaires Behaving Badly* podcast flooded from the speakers.

Philippe squeezed my hand, gave me a little half smile. 'It was you who put all of this together?'

'No. Analise. She's the journalist.'

'Congratulations, madame, on one hell of a show.'

If this didn't get us killed, nothing would. Whether by Daddy Carr or Madame Reynard, it was hard to tell. But dead was dead.

THIRTY-EIGHT

VIE had tapped into the rage of people all over the world. Working class, middle class, wealthy as well. It lit VIE up like fireworks, and the number of people accessing our website was through the roof.

Back home in Kentucky, a bitcoin mine slated for construction in Laurel County lost its permits. The Aussies were considering legislation to make them illegal.

And Olivier's family filed a second lawsuit.

There was an official envelope with the red, blue, and white insignia of France awaiting me at the office, but at least it was not a brown envelope, the sight of which would now nauseate me for the rest of my life. I pulled out the pages, puzzled over the words, and had to use the translate function on my phone.

My in-laws – Olivier's sister, brother, and mother – were suing me for ownership of the NGO which had in its entirety come to Olivier from half-ownership and the estate of his co-owner, then passed down to me as his rightful heir, under the estate laws and jurisdiction of the United States of America. That money had fueled my own NGO. It had fueled VIE. Which had had a lot of attention. And somehow they knew every single euro it was worth.

I took a breath and stared out the balcony, but saw nothing but the darkness in my heart. If they wanted a war, I would give it to them. You cannot understand a family from the outside in, but what I did know was that Olivier was the best of them. And Olivier had loved them and they had treated him badly. Envy? It couldn't have been money, our jobs meant we lived in a sink or swim world, and we sank a lot. Because we lived the life we wanted and didn't follow the rules? They had not come to his funeral, never said one word to me after his death, been radio silent when Leo had been lost for months on Mont Blanc and I thought I'd lost him too.

Did it matter to me? No. They had never been my family. But it hurt Olivier. And that was unforgivable.

So come after me now? Bring it on. I had one simple goal. I was going to burn this bright, hard and fast. I was going to hold them accountable.

I would begin with a counter suit. Olivier's father had died leaving him a share in the family home. That share by law now belonged to me. I was going to get it.

French inheritance turmoil has been known to go on for decades. This one would start right now.

I sent an email to my attorney in Kentucky, copied to my attorney in Paris, and began the fight which would likely still be going on long after I was dead. I had been in France just long enough to see how this often played out. In the south we would call it a grudge match, and my French forever war had begun.

Leo looked up at me and I kissed his head. He was the only one I was not pissed off with these days.

THIRTY-NINE

Two days later, I received a visit from Madame Reynard. She was waiting for me, early, in the little coffee shop that was part of my morning routine. I had not been there since the attack on VIE. It was interesting that everything Sullivan Carr knew about me, she knew too. Or perhaps it was the other way around.

She waved me over to her table. 'Please, sit, and we will have a coffee.'

I thought about it. Sat down.

She ignored me until our coffee came. I waited her out.

She fiddled with her earring. 'You are so stupid sometimes, Junie. A clueless, misguided, little blond coquette from the American South, in so far over her head. Little and small and pointless. You put yourself in danger, you put *Philippe* in danger, a good and intelligent man, who I find very useful sometimes. I don't much care if you get yourself killed – you are naive and stubborn and beyond hope or redemption. But it would be a shame to see Philippe die because of you.

'And so, much as it pains me to do this, I can arrange for a large donation to VIE, but you must back off from Sullivan Carr and let me handle him. If you want to keep your husband alive.'

'How large?'

She took a pen out of her purse, tore a scrap of paper out of a notebook, jotted down a figure, folded the paper in half and handed it to me. I opened it and studied the figures. Her handwriting was atrocious.

'Is that a zero or a decimal point?'

She glanced down at the scrap of paper. 'A zero.'

'And if I say no, are you going to send another death squad to VIE?'

She jerked her head back. 'How could you even think such a thing? You are ridiculous.'

'Not at all. You are at best complicit with Sullivan Carr, at worst you sent the squad yourself, and either way you knew they were coming. If I had any doubt, it is gone. This is a substantial bribe.'

'Junie, I have the police report on everything that happened in the attack. Including that while your staff were being gunned down, you managed to injure yourself by slipping in blood. Oh dear. Did I make you cry?'

I didn't answer.

'But you must think this through. Have you not realized the implication of the video recordings of the death of your staff? The one they took of you before you fell over your dog. Do you think that I would allow such a thing? If I'd set it up, I assure you that, one, you would be dead, and we would not be having this conversation. And two, I would not allow such evidence to be collected. Think. There is only one person who would do such a thing. A billionaire with an ego and a need to see you die.'

'So, you're confirming that Sullivan Carr sent the death squad.'

She tilted her head and did not answer.

I lifted my chin. 'You describe it very well, what happened when my staff was gunned down and I fell over my dog. You've seen the videos. You were involved. Somehow or other, you had a hand in this, because—'

'You cause me trouble? A lot of people cause me trouble. So, be a good little climate activist and take this donation. My NGO supports climate activists; we are horrified by what happened to you, and we will of course make a donation to VIE. And, Junie, there can be many more donations like this. We have a common cause and we should work together.'

'I will not accept your bribe.'

She narrowed her eyes. 'I do not like that word. But you may call it whatever you want so long as you take it.'

'Everything to you is just one more cog in the wheel, and you are as corrupt as the people you go after, using threats, influence, coercion, quid pro quo . . . smug in the delusion that this is how the game must be played, and that the end justifies the means. And all of it taints you, it tempts you, and God knows your ego is way out of hand. Who are you to know what must be done, and who are you to decide, and who are you to offer me money to influence my NGO? I will make mistakes, I will fail and fail again, but I will not get myself fucking compromised by a woman who is at least partially responsible for the death of my staff.'

She gave me a half smile. 'Your language skills are getting better, Madame Lagarde, but your mispronunciation mutes the effect. Any other idiocies you want to share? Otherwise, I must leave; I have an aggressive schedule this afternoon.'

'As a matter of fact, yes, one other thing. This time with you has been an inspiration. You may look forward to seeing your name on the VIE website. I will be adding a new category to our financial disclosures, under the banner "Bribes we have turned down."'

She waved her hand with a smug little smile. 'And what a pleasure that will be.'

'I think maybe not for you, Madame Reynard. But it will be for me.'

FORTY

That night, just before dinner, I had a text from a number I didn't recognize.
This is your brother. Stop ignoring my texts.
I frowned. Had I blocked him? I checked his number. Yes, I had. Months ago. I had been grieving hard for Olivier, and Chris had been a jerk about it, the way people are when they think they know what you need better than you do.

Another text. I checked my contact list. This was Redmond's number, Chris's husband. I really liked Redmond. He and Chris were good together.

If you still want me to be your person for the alarm company for your house, answer your damn phone.

Then it rang. And I answered my damn phone.

'Are you pissed about something?' my brother asked. He sounded genuinely perplexed.

'Yes.'

'Well, if that isn't business as usual. You are the worst about holding a grudge, Junie. So let's move on. Your alarm company called – somebody broke into your house. The police were out there pretty fast. As far as I can tell, nothing is missing. It's not like you have expensive stuff.'

'Well hell.' I wasn't nearly as calm as I sounded. It hits you in your gut, someone invading your home. 'Any damage?'

'They broke two windows and kicked in the back door, but didn't go inside. That was in the middle of the night; the police arrived four minutes later, nobody there. This morning three-one-one code enforcement showed up while I was looking at the damage, saying they had a report that you had not been maintaining the property and the windows had been broken out and there was glass in the driveway. They said they'd had the report two weeks ago. None of this is making sense.'

I sat down on the edge of the bed feeling sick. 'It makes sense to me. It's bloody uncoordinated harassment. They evidently got their dates all mixed up.'

'They? Who's they? You piss somebody off?'
'Daddy Sullivan Carr.'
He was quiet a long moment. 'Well, Junie-bug, why would you do that? Sometimes I think you just look for trouble. You've always been kind of a shit magnet.'
'Don't you ever read the website of my NGO investigative—'
'Your what?'
'VIE.'
'Oh right. No, not really. What does that have to do with Daddy Carr?'
'Never mind.'
'Anyway, they got a video of a guy in your house.'
'I thought you said they didn't go into the house.'
'Not the one this morning. This one was six days ago. He didn't trip the alarm, or break anything, but he did trigger the motion cameras inside. I sent you three texts and called and left a message, and you never got back to me, why is that? Wait, did you block me?'
'*No.* I'm having trouble with my phone.'
He was quiet a moment. 'OK, look, I am texting you the video. For the second time, by the way.'
I waited.
And there he was, waving to the cameras. Le Sorcier. The guy who had grabbed me on the streets of Annecy, threatened me, given me extraordinarily good advice on how to heal my ankle. He could switch careers, go into physical therapy. He was walking up the attic steps in my little downtown cottage in Kentucky, and I wondered what he was going to do in the attic. It was a mess up there. I didn't know what he was looking for, but it would take him years to find it. Even I didn't know what was up there.
Maybe just being there was the point.
'You see that wave? You know this guy, Junie, or is he some kind of ass? Because he didn't take anything.'
'How would you know?'
'Good point, but unless he wants some old photo albums from our childhood . . .'
'Oh God, I hope he didn't take those.'
'Why?'
'All those annual family portraits of us growing up, with bowl haircuts, and hideous sweaters? They can threaten me, they can harass me, but I draw the line at this kind of humiliation.'

'I don't even think you're kidding. But listen, Junie. This guy . . . he looks familiar. I think I saw him at a party once. Years ago. Let me think. Yeah. Back when I broke Gatsby's heart.'

I remembered it the other way around, but I wasn't going to say it. 'Evidently he's been working for the Carr family a long time.'

'Hang on, hang on, let me think. He wasn't working for the Carr family. He *was* family.'

'What, some cousin or something?'

'No, I remember now. Gatsby actually introduced me, said the guy was his big brother from another mother.'

'He's Daddy Carr's son?'

'One of 'em. You be careful with this guy, Junie. I know a lot of the Carrs and I haven't met one yet who wasn't bad news.'

'This one certainly is.'

'What do you mean, do you know him?'

'He's a professional assassin and he's been stalking me.'

'That doesn't sound right to me, Junie. An assassin does not let you know he's hunting you; he kills you outright. What's been going on out there, anyway?'

I told him.

He was quiet for while. I knew it was a lot and I waited him out.

'Why did you stir all this up, Junie? What do you hope to accomplish?'

'I don't *hope* anything. Hope isn't a plan. Somebody has to hold these billionaires accountable.'

'Doesn't mean it has to be you.'

'Chris—'

'Don't hang up, Junie. You need to be really careful.'

'You think?'

'No, listen. Gatsby always told me this brother was really . . . *off*. Really dangerous. That his dad encouraged it, thought it was great, and used his brother for things he wouldn't tell me about. Just said it was some pretty dark stuff, and his dad got a kick out of it. Called him the family asset. He said his brother would do anything for his dad, because, you know – the illegitimate kid who is desperate for a little approval and even, God forbid, love. From his daddy. Gatsby is the same way. Did you see his eyes? How bright they are? Intense?'

'Yes, I have seen his eyes. And this is the real deal? He's Sullivan's Carr's son?'

'From mistress three, who came before wife two, who was Gatsby's mother. So they're close in age. But Luke's mother was French, and she had a falling out with Carr when she was pregnant.'

'His name is Luke? Luke Carr?'

'No, they call him Luke but it's Jean-Luc d'Estaing, which is a lot. His mother's family didn't want anything to do with the kid, so his mother ditched her family and Carr both and raised him in Brittainy. I think she died when Luke was eight, and neither side of the family wanted him. And that's all I know.'

'So he is rejected by his American billionaire side of the family, and his aristocratic French side of the family when he's just eight? No wonder he's so fucked up.'

'Not my problem. Just stay away from him. Look, Junie, I called your contractor guy who renovated the house—'

'Did you? Thanks.'

'He's going to fix what needs to be fixed, settle the issue of the code violations, which are sounding like harassment to me. Also, they hit you with a barking dog violation.'

'Leo is in France.'

'Yeah, exactly. What exactly did you do to piss Carr off so bad?'

'I mean . . . a lot.'

'Give me the short summary version.'

'He blames me for getting him put under a death sentence issued by a terrorist group.'

'Yeah, that would do it.' He went quiet. 'So, Junie, you doing OK? That grief stuff and all?'

'I've learned to carry the weight.'

'How's that police guy doing? That captain?'

'Oh. I married him.'

My brother laughed. 'Well hell, good to catch up. And here we go, another Frenchman in the family. I consider that good news. Maybe bring your fella home sometime; we can have dinner.' Then his voice went dark. 'I think I'm going to give good ol' Gatsby a call. I see him from time to time, but we never really talk. Time for the two of us to reconnect.'

'Don't do that, Chris. Don't get involved in this. It's worse than you think.'

'I'll do as I damn well please. You're still my little sister. And, Junie – unblock me from your phone.'

FORTY-ONE

Le Sorcier was waiting for me in front of Monoprix again. In the heart of Old Town. A central location that I would pass through on my way to just about everywhere. Cafes, restaurants, the pharmacy. Just walking Leo. I was starting to think of it as our place.

He smiled at me, bright-eyed and intense enough to let me know that I would never be safe with this man. 'Let me look at you, madame. You are better. Still limping, of course, but your walk is easier and I do not see so much pain in your face. You are using my method?'

I nodded.

'And your dog, he is matching his steps to yours? How did you train him to do this?'

'I made the suggestion and he figured it out.'

'Eh voilà, a little test for you. To impress me. Ask him to do something that is not a command; *show* me how the two of you seem always to read the other's mind.'

I waved a hand gently to the left and Leo took the invitation and followed, making a wide circle around me. A wave of the hand is the best way to invite a dog; it is gentle, it is a sweet moment of connection, and Leo was always eager to follow my hand just to see what we would do next.

Le Sorcier applauded. 'I would like a dog such as that. And now to business. I do not see you leaving your apartment so much these days. I think you are in pain. Off balance. Afraid you will fall and afraid of me. I have a way we can fix all of these things.'

I had not seen the cane that was resting against the wall behind him, but I saw it now as he held it up. 'About that.'

Simple and sweet. Black with a circling pattern of color – hummingbirds, flowers.

'If I may?' Le Sorcier measured the cane to my waist, and where my hand rested at my side. He adjusted the height. 'Give it a try.'

Leo watched him but stood at my side, curious and calm.

Interesting that. He would read the intent of Le Sorcier. From Leo I knew that the assassin had not come to kill me today.

I leaned my weight on the cane. 'Yes. Perfect. Thank you.'

Le Sorcier was very pleased with himself. 'And now, madame, let's get you off your feet. I invite the two of you to sit with me outside and have a coffee and something sweet. Sullivan Carr has another proposal – no, no, do not have that look on your face, Junie; this is one that I think is good for you to hear. You are both in the same hard place, both afraid for your life, one trying to save the world, the other trying to own it, neither willing to move from your position. I think there is a better way. If you will listen, just listen and hear this out, then I will swear to you a promise that no matter what, I will never hurt your dog.'

'You wouldn't anyway. But you might hurt me.'

'It is, after all, my job.'

'Carr's last proposal was bullshit.'

He sighed. 'This is true. I have something real this time. And some information you need to know. I may be the least of your problems right now.'

'Oh God, don't say that, Jean-Luc d'Estaing.'

'Ah, so you have seen me on the camera in your house.'

'You waved, after all.'

'Your attic is a mess. But the rest I like. Especially the kitchen. You like to cook? Your gas stove is a monster, I like it very much.'

'Yeah, that's not fitting into the little apartment we have here. And I know who you are.'

'Good, now we are both being honest. I have spoken to Gatsby; he warned me you know who I am, and do you know, I have actually met your brother, Chris? He broke Gatsby's heart, you know this?'

'It's not exactly how I heard it.'

He waved a hand just like I had with Leo, and both of us followed him across the street. It was a short walk to Rose des Neiges. The Snow Rose pâtisserie and tearoom. The arched storefront was pink, as were the chairs and tables outside.

Le Sorcier held out a chair for me and I sat carefully, positioning my ankle and my cane. Using it for balance on the walk over had magically taken away my fear of falling. I wondered if his other proposal would be as good.

'Manières au bistrot,' I told Leo. Bistro manners. He settled at my side.

'I will go inside and make the selection. Will Leo have a coffee?'

I tried hard not to smile. 'I will have a coffee. A bowl of water for Leo, please.'

It was the salted caramel macaron that made me shut my eyes tight in ecstasy.

'Did you hear me, Junie?'

'No.'

'When you finish the macaron, I will tell you again. If you listen to all of it, I will get you more.'

'C'est un accord.'

'Your words are correct, but you are pronouncing them wrong. C'est un accord.'

'Shut up.'

He nodded. 'Yes, it annoys you, but someone needs to tell you these things. And now, écoutez. Have you never wondered why Carr – I do not call him my father, and would ask you to do the same – why he has been trying to build a bitcoin mine here, in the Alps?'

'Because he is a spoiled billionaire who doesn't get told no?'

'Yes, but why here? He is not stupid, exactly. It was suggested to him, by someone who convinced him that to do so would be welcomed by France, make him a big-name crypto king with currency investment and bitcoin mines. He will be a big name in the EU. He is competitive with others like him. What did you call him? Tech-broligarch? He loved that, by the way. And he is easy to convince, once the idea is in his head, and his ego is in play. Remember my father, and Gatsby, focus on one thing only – what they do not have. So, this becomes an obsession with him.'

'I already know who convinced him.'

He frowned.

'You are acquainted with Madame Reynard, are you not?'

'Shit.'

'I want more macarons.'

He frowned at me. 'So this is good then, actually. That you know this. But can you prove this?'

I shook my head. 'Not yet. I'm working on it.'

'I see that she has been published on your page of bribes offered. No doubt she loved that.'

'No doubt.'

'And if you could prove beyond doubt who sent the death squad to VIE. Would you publish this?'

'Carr's idea of proof and mine are likely not even close. Let him take it to the media owned by his billionaire friends, which is most of them now. Or let him buy a newspaper or a social media company of his own, if he wants this in the press.'

'It has to be VIE.'

'I won't publish it on VIE. Just because Madame Reynard convinced your father to put in this bitcoin mine does not mean she sent the death squad to our office. I admit I suspected her. A lot. Because I know she *saw* the recordings. But then she made a good point to me. She would not have wanted the deaths recorded. She would not have wanted that evidence to exist. She would not have needed to see it happen. Only a billionaire's ego demands something like that. So. Your father was responsible for the death of my staff. I look forward to reading about his death by snake bite.' I paused. 'Although . . .'

He cocked his head to one side, watching me with a little smile. We were negotiating now.

'I know you went to our office to pick up the burner phones that were used to film the deaths of my staff. And me.'

'But you lived.'

'I did. And that is on video too. And I know you were there to make sure there were no survivors, and that La Puce shut that down. So the proposal is this. You give me those burner phones so we can trace who they went to, so we will have all the "Recording the death of . . ." videos. Did you watch them? Did you see my staff die? Did you see me fall over Leo and slide in the blood?' I studied him. 'Did it upset you or did you watch them with professional detachment?'

'Are you asking what kind of man I am?'

'I'm negotiating for the phones. Give me those and whatever they prove will go up on VIE. And yes. I am also asking what kind of man you are.'

He nodded. 'Then know that I am the kind of man who does his job. Which means I destroyed those phones within fifteen minutes of setting you ever so gently on the couch. I heard La Puce wish you bon courage on my way out.'

I took a breath. I knew it was a longshot, but the disappointment sat heavy. I wanted those phones so bad. But of course they had been destroyed.

He tapped a finger on the table. 'What if there was another way to prove who really sent that death squad? To hold them accountable as you say.'

'I'm listening.'

'My father would like to invite you to meet with him and some of his business associates at the Kentucky Derby in Louisville in May.'

'What, to the high security secret Billionaire's Box right beyond The Mansion and Millionaire's Row? The Billionaires' Bunker, invitation only, for the richest of the rich?' I laughed.

There was no place more exclusive in any sporting event. Staff that didn't belong would get fired for setting foot inside. Security was tighter than a presidential inauguration and one step down from the Super Bowl.

It was a billionaire dream event. Service in The Mansion was high end, including leather tabletops, a Chanel cosmetics counter in the women's lounge, a personal tailor for the men, a seamstress for the women. Fashion at the Derby was for everyone, right down to the infield, and no billionaire wanted any snags in the couture. This was basically an anything-you-want-yes-sir-yes-sir level of service, which made the British royals long for this kind of set up back home in Windsor. Whatever you desired, you would get, from sending out for a rare bourbon, to the billionaire who passed on the food prepared by top chefs flown in from all over the world, to instead demand Chick-fil-A. The kind of things billionaires took for granted, until they didn't get them, then all hell would break loose. Which did *not* happen at the Kentucky Derby, where horses were King, but billionaires came second.

The Kentucky Derby had never been in my price range, unless I wanted to gather on the infield with a hundred thousand drunk college kids. Which I would pass on, even though it was the Derby. The infield was a Wild West show, and no television cameras ever panned the crowd because whatever was going on down there was not for prime time. There was an actual Derby jail, an old underground army bunker left over from the Second World War. You got stuck in there if you got out of hand and stayed in captivity for three hours to sober up. A second infraction earned you big-boy jail.

Le Sorcier handed me a sealed envelope. 'He has provided your invitation and your tickets, of course.'

I looked at the sealed, crisp white envelope. Wondering how much it had cost. A table in the Stakes Room on the fourth floor went for fifty thousand dollars a ticket. Which was nothing compared to this.

I pushed the envelope back across the table.

'Junie. If you will come to the Derby, and meet with Carr, he will give you proof that the entire bitcoin mine and death squad scenario was engineered by Madame Reynard. The meeting where it was actually planned was at the Derby the year before, exactly at the table where you and he will be sitting, and he has it on video. He will give you this evidence, and then the two of you will discuss how to go forward, with VIE breaking the story. He agrees to answer *all* of your questions, let you record the interview on your phone, and hand over the video.' He scrolled down on his phone. 'To show that he is negotiating in good faith, I will show you the segment of the video that has just been sent to the VIE website.'

It was my first look at the Billionaires' Bunker, and there was Madame Reynard, at a long rectangular table, the room thick with men and women smoking cigars, drinking, and having a hell of a time. In the background was the murmur of voices, laughter, the clink of silverware and glasses.

Madame Reynard was wearing an off-the-shoulder fitted sheath dress in white linen her hair in a loose chignon. She looked elegant. Beautiful. And slightly annoyed. The camera had caught Madame Reynard and Sullivan Carr sitting side by side, and I wondered what I had been doing on Derby Day a year ago while all of this was being planned. I had been in France while Madame Reynard had been in Kentucky, which I would not have believed without this video. But that challenging look of disdain on her face was unmistakable.

She took a sip from a three-olive martini and looked steadily at Sullivan Carr.

'Let us work together on this.' I recognized her silky-hard voice. Nobody talked like that but Madame Reynard. It was performance art. 'You let *me* take care of Junie Lagarde and VIE.' She gave him the smile I knew so well. 'And after all, life is getting more and more dangerous for journalists.'

The sound stopped, and Madame Reynard was frozen in time.

Proof. If I had the whole interview, I could take her down for sending the assassins to VIE.

I had to have it.

I reached across the table and took the envelope, tucking it inside my purse.

FORTY-TWO

That afternoon I called an emergency staff meeting, to hear their progress on validating the new scoop for VIE. All they knew right now and what they had been working on was the dynamic with Madame Reynard and Sullivan Carr, and how she had manipulated him. Not such a hard thing to do because billionaires are easy. When they only see what they don't have, you show them what you want them to want. It did not mean you were not responsible for what they did. We would play no sad violins for Carr at VIE.

This new video was going to lead us to gold.

And now it was not so much the billionaires that worried me anymore. They had been in the hands of wealth managers for decades, a symbiotic relationship of expertise and agenda teamed up with the learned helplessness of wealth. That none of them were happy did not interest me. What did interest me was the agenda of the wealth managers. I was unmoved by their little song and dance of modest salaries, and a desire to serve, that they had been telling the world for years. They were fueled by the heady thrill of power. They had information that would make them rich and no doubt they used it. Puppeteers who organized and controlled obscene amounts of money and used it to fuel their virtual takeover of international financial law. Show the billionaires what you tell them to want, show the governments what you tell them to want, and all of them fall into line.

And now a group had formed Les Vipères Emeraudes – show the climate activists what they want, and you will own them too. Maybe they were saving the world. Or maybe they were just taking it. It was up to VIE to find out.

Billionaires and governments had followed them like lambs. There was a part of me that wished their dazzle of saving the world was true.

Nothing about this could even be discussed with my staff. Not if I wanted to keep my husband alive.

For now, I was interested in what my staff thought of my decision to go to the Kentucky Derby. A decision made on gut instinct. Whisk me across the ocean at their convenience, dangle exclusive admission to the world of bespoke horse racing in my face, and my automatic reaction was to say 'hell no.'

But give me proof of Madame Reynard setting up the death squad that attacked VIE . . . It was not possible to say no. She was dangerous. She had to be taken out. And her mockery of me for slipping in blood played in an endless loop in my mind.

I wanted my staff to chime in. The young ones were hard to predict, but they were not just essential, they saw the world a different way, had fresh opinions on how far we should go, and when we should hold back. They were going to be the future of VIE, but they were a guiding force right now. They had not grown up with the beaten-down lessons of the generation before, that the mean parts of the world had to be taken in stride. If calling bullshit on this meant they were snowflakes, VIE embraced it. Snowflakes are more beautiful than bitcoin mines.

The Kentucky Derby. I could see up close and in person this watering hole for the extreme elite. There they would be catered to, and safe, like toddlers on a padded playground with an army of nannies to cater to their every need. They would not like that analogy. They would call it *bespoke*. They had their own language, the very rich. And I could use them to take down Madame Reynard.

The question, of course . . . was it smart? Could I do this and keep my own agenda, or was I falling down their rabbit hole?

It was never hard to get Analise into the office. What was hard was getting her to go home. Right now, I needed her insight. Something this important was always a joint decision. I would need her go-ahead.

But first of all, I wanted everyone together. We were small. We were under threat. We were not starry-eyed and unrealistic; we did not have hope because hope was not a plan. We had a steady purpose. But we lived with the ongoing ripples of the attack that had changed us forever. I was the guiding hand; Analise was the expert. All decisions would be made together.

FORTY-THREE

Whenever I walked into the office now, I saw so many things, layers upon layers. I could see all of them, the people I worked with at VIE. Some of them living, some of them dead, how excited we were the day we moved in, the outraged laughter the day Timothée announced he was Master of Tech, bragging how his sister was even better, that he was trying to get her in the office to meet us; he wanted to show her off. Bloodstains on the wall, Leo curled up in his favorite chair. Lilou crying softly in the kitchen when she thought she was alone. Matis treating us to the daily fart jokes we had come to expect along with coffee, and the fading bouquets laid at the door by a city that folded us in and loved us, no matter how much trouble we brought.

And the ever-present baguettes on the kitchen counter delivered regularly and at random by Bigfoot, who was becoming the VIE mascot. Leo was security detail on staff.

Soon we would have a baby, too.

Analise was sitting in the office rocking chair, that we'd had delivered just three days ago. She looked well rested, calm, and happy to be at work. I had wondered how she would react to the Derby decision. I had emailed the staff, told them what was up, called a meeting. Analise was quiet and sitting still, which meant she was thinking. Analise thinking was always a good thing.

We were making a baby nursery in a corner of the office, at her request. She was planning an extended maternity leave and wanted to be free to come into the office when she wanted, to keep up the podcasts if possible, without any pressure to work or not work. She expected days where she would curl up with her baby and be too tired to move. What she wanted was options. Not to be slotted into an agenda she could not possibly predict. She wondered out loud and often why she was expected to make decisions when the very definition of her life was going to be unpredictability. And was this not like retirement, where people are expected to decide how long they will live and how much they will need when lifespan and the cost of living cannot be known?

I had zero experience with this sort of thing, but what I could do was make sure that at VIE she would not have that pressure.

And the baby had recently acquired a name. Hubert.

As well as Analise, the rest of my staff had also been assembled and was waiting the minute I walked into the VIE office. They'd had intense discussions since I had brought them up to date earlier. They'd seen the video of Madame Reynard, and there had been an intense and heated debate on my invitation to the Derby.

Analise had also given them the story of Empress, and the thing they were most excited about was my horse, and I had been getting a stream of excited texts.

Could they come and see her and feed her a carrot and pet her head? They had not ever had a chance to meet a horse.

I had said yes and promised to hold a barn party, once Hubert was born and Analise and Stéphane were open to visitors. I knew very well that horses had a way of healing the heart. Empress would become the emotional support animal of VIE, second only to Leo, who was as integrated into the ebb and flow of the office as I was.

Lilou smacked a hand on her desk and called the meeting to order.

'We have discussed it among the staff, Junie, and decided that you must on no account go to the Kentucky Derby and meet with Sullivan Carr and his pig buddies. He does not dictate to you. You may offer him a meeting here in our offices at VIE, which all members of the staff will attend. We want him to see the banner on the wall, and the bullet holes, and sit in the room where there are still bloodstains under the paint.'

I looked to Analise. 'What do you think?'

She bit her lip. 'We must not be ordered around, but we must not let our egos get in the way of business.'

There was always that.

'So, you think I should go?'

'The question is whether you think this is legitimate. I think we cannot ignore the chance to look at the evidence Carr says he has. If we can prove who sent the death squad to VIE, that would be worth everything, I think.'

'The video is legit,' Lyam said.

Lilou jumped up out of her chair. 'We know who sent the death squads. It was both of them, Madame Reynard and Sullivan Carr.'

'Knowing isn't proof,' Analise said, rocking fiercely in her chair.

Lilou paced around the room. 'To send Junie there is nothing but catering to their demands. You judge them by their patterns of behavior. And that means do not go, Junie. They will have an agenda, and it will not be good.'

'Understood,' I said. 'OK. Anything new? Bring me up to date.'

'A new feature,' Lilou said. 'Suggested by Matis. Tell Junie what you want to do.'

He leaned forward, eyes bright. 'We have gotten so many pictures and emails from people who live with bitcoin mines, people recovering from the out-of-control storms, and the heat that becomes dangerous, and feel forgotten in the world. So, we invite more of this and post regularly. To give them a voice and let them know we are all together and they are not forgotten.'

Lyam gave a slow whistle. 'Good one, Matis.'

'About the cows and methane—'

'No fart jokes, Matis,' Lilou said. 'At least not outside of the office,' she added, when he looked crushed.

But then he smiled. 'It is now time for Lyam to show you his idea for a new VIE logo.' He pounded a drumroll on his desk.

With a click of the keyboard that told me Lyam had been waiting for his moment, it went up in all its glory on the monitor on his desk, to cheers, whistles, and applause.

I laughed out loud.

'Take it to a vote,' I said.

Unanimous.

Bigfoot eating a baguette, under a banner with *Billionaires Suck* crossed out in red, and underneath, also in red: *Bigfoot était là.*

Bigfoot was here.

Lyam looked at me with eyes shining. 'I will have one made as a banner to hang in the office. Next to the one with bullet holes.'

And that was the moment I decided to go to the Kentucky Derby. For sure. A decision I would keep to myself.

'OK. Listen up. I have an announcement to make.'

Everyone looked up, edgy and worried.

'A *good* announcement,' I said. 'I have rented a new office for VIE, and we can move in whenever we want. I have done a shitload of negotiating and paperwork, and have signed a three-month lease, paid in advance.'

Cheers. Whistles. Applause. Yet again. My staff was nothing if not exuberant.

'But wait,' Matis said. 'I do not mean to be rude, Junie, but this is a lot of effort for a three-month lease that you could get at any Airbnb.'

'Yes, but. That is how long it will take for VIE to *buy* the apartment. My offer has been made and accepted, it should take three months for the sale to go through, and then we will own the apartment, as insurance against billionaires who want to buy it out from under us. I was an accountant in another life, and I intend to make our new place billionaire-proof.'

Matis and Lyam did a high five. 'I was afraid I would have to start working again in my mother's basement,' Matis said.

'Not much of a commute, since that is where you live,' Lyam said. 'Where is it, this new office? Is it far from here? There will never be a location as good as this. But of course, I am sure you have found a place that is very good.'

I stood up. 'Follow me.'

I led them down the hallway, to the heavy plastic sheeting that covered the door La Puce had made between the office and the apartment next door. It had not been fixed, because the owner of the apartment and Carr's management both felt this repair was not their responsibility. A dispute that could drag on for months, if not years.

I pulled the sheeting away. Balled it up. Tucked it under my arm.

'This is ours?' Analise said. She charged in, no doubt looking for the best place for her desk and Hubert's nursery. I let Leo off the leash and he trotted in behind her.

I waved a hand. 'Go explore,' I told them. Everyone thundered in except Lilou.

She wandered back into the front room, and sat on the edge of her desk, hands over her face. 'I don't want to leave him behind, my brother. He died here,' she said, voice so tight it hurt to hear.

'I know.'

'And to think that Sullivan Carr will own this.'

'I know. But one thing I know about your brother, Lilou. He will be with you wherever you go.'

She looked up, eyes glistening, and nodded. Gave me a quick hug. 'Please don't go to the Derby,' she said softly, then turned away and ran after the others.

I sat down in my leather chair to think.

And just for a moment, I caught a glimpse of him. Lilou's brother, Timothée, Master of Tech, standing at the edge of the kitchen. A smile, a shimmer, and he was gone.

I made coffee, gave them time. It was not long before Analise arrived, walking like her back hurt, and settling into her rocking chair again. Lilou headed to the kitchen for coffee, and Lyam and Matis thundered in one after the other, with Leo barking behind them.

'I have a question for you, Junie.' Lyam skidded to a halt in front of my chair, Matis close on his heels. 'And it is this – are you not afraid to meet with Sullivan Carr at the Derby?'

'I will be very safe,' I said. 'But don't take my word for it. Pull up the Churchill Downs website and take a look. Because the security there is obscene. Look at the list of the things you cannot take inside. The metal detectors. The National Guard posted along the backside. And to get to the Billionaire's Bunker you have to go through The Mansion that is invitation only. No one goes inside unless escorted by their own personal concierge. They meet you when you arrive and escort you to the elevator, and hand you a glass of champagne to drink while the elevator takes you to the fifth floor. There are people who work there day in and day out and don't know what it looks like. There are people who don't even know it's there. Millionaires Row a floor down is nothing compared to the Billionaires' Bunker.'

'But in truth, Lyam? No, I'm good with this. I will take Leo. I'm actually looking forward to it.'

Lyam smiled. 'Because we are spies in plain sight. This is our own James Bond movie. *Derby Royale.*'

'No,' Matis said. '*Annecy Royale*. We must keep this French.'

'Take a vote,' I said.

Unanimous for *Annecy Royale*.

I realized how very tired I was.

'So long,' I told them with a wave, a phrase they loved for being so very American. Au revoir left them cold.

Analise caught up to me as I headed out the door. We stopped at the top of the stairs.

'You've decided?'

'I can't resist. I have to go. If we can prove who sent the death squads . . '

She nodded. 'You really are not afraid?'

'Hell no, I can't wait. But keep this between us. If anyone asks, I'm still thinking. And make sure the staff know how confidential this is.'

'They know. But I will remind them. What will Philippe say?'

'Philippe? Yeah. I'm not telling him.'

FORTY-FOUR

The meeting with VIE had gone on late, and when I got home, Philippe was asleep on the couch. He looked exhausted, disheveled, deep lines in his face. I wanted to trace those lines with my fingertips and kiss him gently on the mouth. I let him sleep while I gave Leo his dinner, then sat beside him on the couch, holding two glasses of red wine.

He sat up, smiled at me, ran a hand over his face.

'You look exhausted,' I told him. 'Are you hungry?'

'Getting that way. What do you want for dinner?'

I thought about it. 'Pizza from Queen Mamma sounds good.'

He took his glass of wine, looking worried. 'You have something on your mind, Junie. You have not called my ex-wife again?'

'No, no, not that.' I set my glass down. It amazed me that my husband knew in an instant when I was hiding something. 'It's just . . . I don't want anything to happen to you. When I lost Olivier . . .' I trailed off.

All of this was true, after all.

He leaned close and kissed me. 'Nothing will happen to me but that I go and get pizza and be right back.' He gave me a half smile. 'Unlike you, who can actually not find her way through Old Town, I promise not to get lost.'

His phone rang. He gave it a look and did not answer. 'I will be back as soon as I can.'

He gave me a quick, hard kiss, grabbed his jacket, moving fast and furious down the stairs. I wondered if he'd remember the pizza.

It was Leo who woke me, nose to the balcony door giving a hard huff. I had fallen asleep on the couch. I looked at my phone. Philippe had not called. He had been gone over three hours.

Leo barked hard, and I grabbed my cane, but the ankle felt steady and my balance was good. Soon I would not need it. Leo pawed the balcony door and I opened it to the darkness, knowing I was illuminated by the light behind me in the apartment. I thought of myself as a target these days.

The floor of the balcony was cold through my thick white socks and I held tight to the rail. Leo was there beside me, paws up on the railing. I put a hand on his neck. Told him to hush.

I saw them. Two men talking. Philippe and La Puce, who looked up to see Leo and me on the balcony. Philippe carried three pizza boxes from Queen Mamma, which was right around the corner at 20 Rue du Pâquier. I was starving now, and this was my favorite pizza in the whole world.

Philippe blew me a kiss and waved, then both men moved out of sight, and I heard them thundering up the stairs.

Leo got the zoomies the minute they came through the door, trailing cold air and the smell of pizza. He gave Philippe kisses, and when La Puce pounded his chest and said, 'Come to me, you beautiful boy,' he gave him the leap of affection and La Puce got a doggie kiss.

'Is it me you want or the pizza?' La Puce said.

Philippe got plates and opened the square white boxes. One margherita pizza – basil, oregano, parmesan and mozzarella. The Queen, with white ham, mushrooms, and olives, and the Tartufo, with black truffle cream, ham, mushrooms, and olives. I went to the refrigerator and pulled out three beers. Sylvanus Blonde from the local Brasserie du Mont Blanc.

They were easy together, La Puce and Philippe. They exchanged looks.

'What?' I said, chewing pizza. My ankle was feeling pretty good, my upset stomach was a thing of the past, and I was going to eat as much pizza as I could hold.

La Puce had his elbows on the table, beer in one hand, slice of pizza in the other. 'I understand that Sullivan Carr is going to invite you to the Derby, Junie.' He gave me a sideways look.

'Where did you hear that?'

'The Brit. Carr's wealth manager. Who was instructed to get you the invitation and the ticket, in hopes that you would meet with Carr and his billionaire buddies at the Kentucky Derby.'

'Why would they want me there?' I asked.

Philippe was watching me. He knew me way too well.

'I do not know their agenda,' La Puce said. He wolfed down the slice of pizza, and I pushed the open box closer, so he could get another slice. 'The Brit is worried because Carr got lofty with him and just said do as you are told. Something the Brit did not much like, though with Carr it happens a lot.'

'Do you think Carr suspects the Brit is a Viper?'

La Puce shook his head. 'He would be fired by now if that were true. There are plenty of other wealth managers who would like to take his place. The Brit has family that is royalty adjacent, and Carr loves that. He will not believe that the Brit is a Viper.'

'He is right though, Junie, and you will not go to the Derby,' Philippe said.

'Do not lay down the law with me, Philippe.'

He gave me a serious look. 'You have been invited?'

'No,' I said. It surprised me how easily I lied. Something I had always been good at.

La Puce gave me a steady look. 'If you have truly not yet been invited, you will be. I tell you this again, Junie. *Do not go.*'

'Do not do that,' Philippe said. 'If you tell her not to do something, she will always do the opposite. Let me know if they invite you, Junie, and you and I will talk.' He squeezed my hand and I pulled it away.

Leo looked up at La Puce in adoration.

'Your dog, he loves me.'

'Only because you are feeding him pizza.'

I put two more pizza slices on a plate, got a beer, and headed into the bedroom. Closed the door. Leo followed me, scratched, and I let him in.

Loyalty.

I heard Philippe and La Puce talking in low voices.

I had zero interest in what they were saying. I did not like them arriving and telling me what to do. As if I did not run VIE; as if I had not been through hell, as if they had the right.

My husband has once again disrespected me in my kitchen.

French children eat Oreo cookies for breakfast every single day. You will not go to the Derby, but of course we can talk about it, before I tell you no again.

I thought not.

I gave Leo a generous bite of pizza. Looked down at him. 'Do you want to go with Mama to the Kentucky Derby? Will you promise not to bark at the horses? You can bark at the billionaires instead. We will be in the bunker behind The Mansion and I hear the food there is very good.'

FORTY-FIVE

The fallout that I knew was coming was literally on my doorstep when I got back from the barn after spending the morning with Empress. Grooming her. Taking her for a walk. Feeding her and Cooper carrots I had bought at the market that week. A journey I would make again and again.

A worried Eugene, a good friend to me and Olivier, who ran Chez Eugene on the ground floor of the building where I lived, scrambled up the stairs after me. I had shared this apartment with Olivier. Now I shared it with Philippe.

I shed my barn boots in the hallway and opened the front door to let Eugene inside. He had the worried look I saw on him more often than not. Running a small bistro meant trouble every day, so it didn't necessarily have anything to do with me.

Except this time, it did.

'Junie, an odd thing has happened.' He held out a tightly wrapped package with my name and address on the side. 'This was delivered to my restaurant this morning to give to you personally. By a man in Venetian costume, so it had to be one of those Vipères, who cannot get it through their heads that the Carnival has been over for weeks. It made me angry that he gave me this command to deliver this, but I thought I better go along. You are in some kind of trouble with these guys?'

'Toujours.' Always.

He nodded. Exactly what he expected. 'Keep your Leo close. Does Philippe know about whatever this is?'

'I will tell him.' Maybe. Maybe not.

He nodded with the relief of a man who has done his duty, handed me the package, reminded me that tomorrow night was his night for poulet rôti, roast chicken, and Philippe and I would be there, oui?

'Oui.'

'Bien.' He promised to have some chicken cooked carefully for Leo, whose stomach was never going to be happy with rich sauces and spices, though Leo might say otherwise. It is hard to tell a dog no, he said firmly. But, Junie, you must.

I admitted it was always a problem for me.

And one other thing. A man had come round to find me and asked Eugene to request a lunch meeting at Brasserie l'Abbaye, on Rue du Pâquier, a pedestrian street around the corner from Le Splendid Hotel. He would stay and wait for me there until two.

It was just past noon. I had plenty of time.

'Who was this guy?'

'Oui, yes, I ask him this. He said to say the man from Monoprix.' Le Sorcier.

I thanked him, and he gave me a suspicious look, then gave up when I did not explain. He must go; it was the beginning of the two-hour lunch hustle, and his wife should not be left on her own, though today the business was slow.

But why this Monoprix man would suggest lunch at l'Abbaye when I could have just come downstairs, where he, Eugene, could keep an eye on things, he did not know, because everyone knew that I was followed by one kind of trouble after another.

'He should have arranged it that way, Eugene. You are absolutely right.'

He paused and looked at me over one shoulder. 'You always tell me, Junie, that you like the quiet life.'

'I do. But it will never happen if I don't stop pissing everybody off.'

'You will never stop,' he said with a laugh. 'And I think you never should.'

As soon as I heard Eugene's footsteps fading down the stairs, I shut the door and opened the package, with wave after wave of dread in the pit of my stomach.

The emerald of death had arrived for me.

Why, I did not know. It made no sense. Up until now, the Vipers had been protecting me. La Puce had made sure Analise got home safe.

But. The Brit, an influential wealth manager Viper, would know that I had not only gotten the invitation to the Derby, but that I had accepted it. And directly after that, La Puce had shown up on my doorstep with pizza and a warning not to go.

Evidently in their cost-benefit analysis I was now a liability. Just the chance that I would talk to Sullivan Carr had brought the threat of death. Why didn't they want me to go, I wondered? What didn't they want me to find out?

It only made me more determined. Philippe had been right about one thing: if you tell me not to do something, I am compelled to do it. And if Carr had evidence, I was going to get it. Provided I lived that long.

As for the emerald . . . I could always sell it. I wondered how much it was worth.

FORTY-SIX

There was just enough time for me to put my barn boots back on and keep Leo close beside me for a snake hunt all through the apartment. In case the Vipers were moving fast. And I thought of Le Sorcier telling me that Sullivan Carr continually had his home fumigated, and slept without blankets, which suddenly seemed like a good idea.

But I had Leo. He had a good nose. He was lethal to snakes and an old hand at killing them. He would match the strike of the head with a swift lunge of his own to take their measure, then move in for a quick slit of their throat with a tooth. Which didn't slow them down. He would strike and slice again and again, then pick them up by the tail and bash them into the ground over and over until they were dead. Then he would bring them to me with the enormous pride of a dog who has done a very good job. Only once had he brought me a snake that wasn't quite dead, and my scream brought him running back. He was as apologetic as he knew how to be, grabbed the snake and slammed it into the ground until it was more than dead, then apologized to me with kisses and kisses.

There was nothing I could do to dissuade him when he scented a snake. I did not consider him immune to snake bites, but so far even the emergency call did not tear him away from battling a snake to the death. It was a Red Zone event. German Shepherd overruled.

If there was a snake in the house, or even the building, Leo would know.

FORTY-SEVEN

The idea of a snake in the apartment was enough to make me look forward to meeting Le Sorcier for lunch. There would not likely be snakes at l'Abbaye. And I wanted Jean-Luc's thoughts on my little emerald gift, a promise of attractions to come. Les Vipères Emeraudes always liked to kill you to your face.

I wrapped the package back up and stuck it in a cluttered kitchen drawer. Inside I found Olivier's framed picture of his family in Provence. I would toss it in a dumpster on my way to lunch. Small pleasures.

Leo, who had sniffed horse scent all over me with a great deal of interest and disapproval, was happy to be leashed up and on the move. He kept a bouncy trot as we went down the street and around the corner to l'Abbaye.

Le Sorcier was waiting for me on the terrace, under the white awning that covered the sidewalk like a tent. It had rained, but it was dry inside. He was at a table next to the pavement, the backs of the metal chairs covered in white furry throws as they always were at l'Abbaye, and he was not alone.

Madame Reynard sat across from him.

I gave him a grim look, and he shrugged and waved me in. He did not look any happier to have her there than I was. I wondered what the fuck she was up to now. It couldn't be good.

Her glorious wavy highlighted blonde hair, which I envied more than I liked to admit, was twisted in the kind of effortless chignon I could never achieve. She was wearing a snug emerald-green suit, with a crisp pink tailored blouse and a string of fat white pearls. Dammit, I wanted those pearls. I supposed I could offer to trade her an emerald.

She wore high heels and I wore adorable half boots. Score one for me, looking good while walking over cobblestones.

'High heels, Madame Reynard?' I said as I settled at the table next to Jean-Luc. 'You don't think that is showing your age just a bit?'

Jean-Luc leaned close and gave me fond kisses on both cheeks, which annoyed me. Madame Reynard looked from one of us to the other, making calculations in her head. Whatever she concluded, she did not like, and this was not at all what she expected. But then she smiled. She always does.

'How interesting to see the two of you together,' she said. 'You seem to have some kind of connection which I did not expect. It makes what I am about to say so much . . . so much more *difficult*. For the two of you.'

Jean-Luc and I exchanged looks.

'Pardon me for being inquisitive, but I understand, Junie, that you have been invited by Sullivan Carr to the Kentucky Derby, with exclusive and by-invitation-only admission to the Billionaires' Bunker.'

'That's true,' I said. 'I understand you've been there yourself.'

Madame Reynard narrowed her eyes. 'And this invitation was issued by Monsieur d'Estaing here, who if you did not know, is the son of Sullivan Carr?'

The look Jean-Luc gave her was lethal.

She gave me a smug look and tilted her head to one side. 'That comes as a surprise, Junie?'

Jean-Luc's eyes were bright, which meant he was cataloging ways to kill her. 'Of course she knows. Junie and I are old friends. Our brothers used to date. We are almost family, Junie and I.' He turned to me with a grimace. 'You know, Junie, my father has never invited *me* to the Kentucky Derby, and I have always wanted to go.'

Madame Reynard smacked her hand down on the table. 'In fact, Monsieur d'Estaing, I am sure you will be there this year. Your father has let me know that you will do your job. Which is to ensure that Junie goes to the Derby and if anything happens to him between now and then, you will—'

'Kill her?'

She shrugged. 'So sorry, Junie. And poor Philippe, who will lose a wife so young. How is Philippe, by the way?'

'Oh, your name came up just last night.'

'Is that so?'

'Yes, he said he was going to destroy you. When he could find the time.' And he would have said it if he knew what I knew.

The look she gave me went from shock to venom.

'I do not know why you are willing to meet with Carr. No doubt he has made a promise to you for information or money for VIE, or maybe he is trading you information about other billionaires so you will lay off him. But I know this man and he will not deliver. It is not smart of you to go. You are taking a very big risk.'

I wondered if she knew that Carr had promised proof that she had sent the death squads to VIE.

Her lips went tight. 'I see you are not convinced. I have warned you and you will not listen. Try and survive the Derby, Junie, though I think that is unlikely. You will not have Les Vipères Emeraudes to watch over you this time.'

'I am already on my own. I got a package today from the Vipers. An emerald. A death threat. Maybe I am safer in Kentucky.'

'And I received one as well,' Jean-Luc said. 'So, it seems to me that they do not want either of us at the Derby. I wonder why the Vipers do not want Junie to talk with my father. Do you have any insight on that?'

I had never seen her taken by surprise before and it threw her. 'Do not do this, Junie.'

I did not answer.

She headed out, heels clattering softly, and I admit I envied a woman who could wear high heels over cobblestones like I wore boots.

Jean-Luc watched her go. 'I think that one does not like you, Junie.'

'Perceptive as always.'

'And you got a little package today, just like me?'

'If you mean an emerald of death, why yes, I did.'

'And they too do not want you to go to the Derby. If VIE can prove it was Madame Reynard who sent the death squads—'

'Yeah. Your father is off the hook.'

'Showy bastards. It is unprofessional to telegraph what you will do next.' He opened a menu. 'Let's have some food. I propose we share a pot of mussels, which will come with bread to dip in the juices and more frites than you can eat. I myself will manage. We will have also a couple of beers, and afterwards, if you are very good, we will order the pastries for dessert, and you will eat one and close your eyes in ecstasy like you do with the caramel macaroon.'

'I am feeling pulled in two directions, Jean-Luc. If Madame Reynard does not want me to go, I think I should. If the Vipers sent me a death threat, after protecting me all this time . . . then evidently they don't want me to go badly enough to kill me. It's a hell of a turnaround.'

'They have sentenced my father to death for all the world to see. They will not allow you to prove otherwise.'

'If your father truly has the proof.'

'I think you will have to go and find out.' He smiled at me. 'Another day, another death threat.'

The beers came quickly. For which I was grateful.

FORTY-EIGHT

One did not risk the snags of international travel when you had plans to attend the Kentucky Derby. It is held always the first Saturday in May, the big and final event in the Kentucky Derby Festival, which goes on for two weeks, but keeps the city of Louisville in thrilled chaos for the entire month of April. The run for the roses has never missed a year and the winning horse is crowned with a blanket of red roses, one for every thoroughbred who has run in the race. The last time I watched the Derby the number of roses was up to 564.

Leo and I were on a flight to Kentucky the last week of April. Because he was my hearing assistance dog, he was welcomed on our United Airlines flight from Geneva to Cincinnati, Ohio, with a layover at Dulles in Washington DC. We had the bulkhead seats in Premium Economy, row 20, middle seats D and E – the only place on the plane big enough for a hundred-pound German Shepherd to be comfortable stretched out on the floor. We left Switzerland for Cincinnati on April 29th. We did not want to chance missing the most exciting two minutes in sport.

We landed a little before seven PM, rented a car, and I drove us home to stay in the little cottage in Lexington that I had shared with Olivier. We had been planning to sell it when he died.

On the night before the Derby, though, we would be staying in Louisville, in the Brown Hotel, and our exclusive Derby package would include transportation to and from Churchill Downs where the Derby was run.

Parking . . . impossible on Derby day. Traffic . . . impossible for the entire Derby week. It was worth the price of the hotel to get to and from the track.

Some years the horses raced in pouring rain, in a race known as a mudder. Some horses loved it, some did not, and all of them slipped and slid to the point where I could barely stand to watch. This year was going to be sunshine and cool breezes, topped off by high-end bourbon. If you don't like your bourbon neat or on the rocks, skip the mint julep because the track bartenders do not have the time to make it properly. Go for the bourbon slushie instead.

I had not been back to Lexington in almost two years. How strange it was to be here. The one-hour-fifteen-minute drive from Cincinnati was eerily familiar, even when the sky went from light to dark.

The house I will always love is at the nexus of urban blight, the warehouse distillery bourbon district, and an up-and-down historic neighborhood, where you learn that rundown houses do look better when they're old. It is a vortex of gayborhood, college students in a warren of apartments in big old houses, the occasional meth lab, and a sprinkling of power couples, artists, writers, and – rare for a neighborhood like this – a very small contingent of young families in the stroller stage with an urban warrior gene.

One mile away, as we made our way down Newtown Pike, Leo began to whine and look out the window. He knew exactly where he was.

The small Queen Anne Victorian cottage sat with grace and admirable confidence at the top of a hill and the driveway was steep. I have found that houses built in the 1800s are not just charming; they're tough.

Olivier and I did extensive renovations, and the house was beautiful to me. It had that downtown treasure of a small yard behind a high fence, with an outdoor fireplace made of stone, and a garden. Leo loved that backyard with all his heart, and he used to keep a treasure trove of balls gathered between the wicker chair where Olivier used to sit and my porch swing where I liked to stretch out. Forensic accounting is not as cyclical as the rest of the economy, just the opposite in fact, and the house was a bargain. I bought it in the middle of a recession on pretty good terms, so that we would always have a safe haven to return to while Olivier and I rambled all over the world.

And now it was my connection to a life I was homesick for. When it was Olivier and me and Leo against the world. A sanctuary that kept us safe, so long as we were careful backing out of our driveway into the street.

Part of me wanted to sell it. Part of me could not bear to let it go. When you lose your husband, you hold tight and hard to everything that could be a connection, from houses, to leather jackets, to old socks. None of these things bring your beloved back.

The feelings never end, but I have learned to live with them in softness. When we pulled into the driveway, Leo was beside himself with excitement, and when I had him safely tucked away in the backyard, the gate shut and locked, I freed him from his service vest and the double set of leashes and let him run.

He raced through the yard, nose to the ground, barking in outrage at a squirrel, and immediately found a worn-out treasure trove of his favorite balls beneath my porch swing, along with a tattered and battered stuffed animal. Cool Kat the llama, rain worn, and covered in leaves and dirt, had been waiting to be loved for going on two years. Leo had a new one in France. I sat on the porch swing, threw balls and watched him run, and wondered why I had been so long coming back.

Wishing Philippe was there. Missing Olivier.

That night I built a fire in the fireplace while Leo chased squirrels, then settled in Olivier's chair, ball tucked tightly on the left side of his mouth. I fed him his dinner outside, which he loved, and drank a glass of wine.

Being back at the house brought light, and an odd peace and closeness to Olivier. I was falling back in love with my little cottage all over again.

Later, when I did a load of laundry, and heard the dryer chime, so familiar, the background noise of years I had spent with Olivier, I cried, rambled through the house, feeling yet again like a ghost, caught between the living and the dead.

And then Philippe called, and I was once again OK. He thought I was still in France. I wanted to show him where I was, take him on a phone video tour of the house, of the embers still glowing in the fireplace outside, of Leo running wild through the backyard. But we were deep in deception, Philippe and I.

'I wish I was home with you,' he told me, voice thick with fatigue.

'I wish you were too. Still no way to get free?' What a liar I was. Letting him think I was at home in our little apartment, pining away.

'Not possible.'

Madame Reynard was taking heavy fire, and Philippe was working to bring her down. There were meetings and secretive strategy sessions with the judge and the politicians who were outraged at being held hostage by wealth managers who were threatening to pull a massive amount of investments out of France. Philippe was pinned down in Metz. The timing could not have been better. He'd left two days before I caught my plane.

After talking to Philippe, I cooked a quick pasta in my perfect kitchen with the farmhouse sink, and the Wolf gas stove, opening windows to let the spring breezes in. Leo was stretched out and dozing on the worn leather couch. How strange to remember the nights that Olivier, Leo and I were piled on that couch together.

Once the dishes were cleared, I took a glass of wine to the living room and settled beside Leo on the couch. I was happy to be home, and it wrapped around me in a little glow, and everything I saw that used to annoy me made me smile. This gave me a twinge of guilt. Like I was cheating on France.

I cleaned the guitar that had sat in a case in a corner of the living room. Gave it new strings. I liked the way it felt, snug in my lap, silent so long in my little cottage.

I was hearing music in my head. Milonga de Amor, that drifted and faded into new music, that only existed in my head. Something I was working through.

I took a sip from the glass of wine that sat on the battered sixties coffee table, with the sides that go up and down, scratched wood, the coffee table I grew up with, where my brother and I played endless games of monopoly, that I stole from my father's house, the day after my mother died.

It wrapped itself around me, the life I used to have, but I had cried already, then washed my face with a thick cool cloth, kicked off my shoes, and slid into my oldest softest jeans, rummaged in the closet until I found one of Olivier's white dress shirts with frayed cuffs that I rolled back.

I sat with the stillness and closed my eyes, listening to the music in my head. Jesse Cook, playing 'Into the Dark.'

And then that faded and the only music I heard was mine.

FORTY-NINE

The Mansion at Churchill Downs is the most exclusive area in all of sport, and it is only open for two races – the Oaks and the Derby. It is a secret Billionaire's Bunker that most people are not aware of, for the elite who hold their noses up at Millionaire's Row. There are no signs to follow and there are people who work at Churchill Downs who do not know it exists. It has the best views of the grandstand and the track. Celebrity chefs were flown in, as was wait staff from New York, used to dealing with celebrities. The guests expected an over-the-top experience, and they got it.

With an average of 170,000 people attending the Derby, it takes an average of six hundred people manning seven kitchens to handle the food. Twelve semi-trucks to bring in the food. Tens of thousands of pounds of meat to feed the racegoers.

In The Mansion the menu included sauteed greens and beans topped with shaved black truffle, which went for two thousand dollars a pound. There was caviar, mini salmon burgers with lemon aioli, crisp bacon sourced by local farmers, grilled lemon and tomatoes on brioche. Argentinian red shrimp and grits with white wine, garlic and parsley. Prepared-to-order dishes were always available.

Leo and I were driven from the Brown Hotel to Churchill Downs and dropped off at the entry gate. He was looking at the people who were looking at him. There had been extensive renovations since I'd last been there. There are no racetracks in the world like there are in Kentucky. Churchill Downs, with its white tiers and spires, looks like a wedding cake.

I had bought a pretty dress. A silky black sundress with red poppies, thin delicate straps, and a bit of ruffle at the hemline to flow and sway a few inches below my knees. I wore black calf-high boots, with a very low heel so I could walk. Comfortable shoes were essential on race days – the concession stands sold flip-flops at fifty bucks a pair, and they always sold out. Heels would kill you by the end of the day.

It was chilly out, though the sun was making my cheeks glow

pink. I wore black tights, and a small three-quarter-length silky black sweater with pearl buttons. Leo had a new bow tie, racing green, with tiny brown horses. My hat – and at the Derby there is always a hat – was mini tea party style, made of black linen with fine mesh, big white pearls circling the brim. A small, elegant black feather bouquet sat snugly at the back. It was exquisite and delicious and the little tag that came with it categorized it as a vintage fascinator. I had pearl-rimmed black sunglasses to match.

I loved this hat so much that I was going to take it back with me to France and wear it in Annecy while I walked Leo in Old Town every day it didn't rain. And he would wear his racing bow tie.

The hats were the best part of the Derby, second only to the horses. Many Derby milliners worked full-time just to have enough hats for the Derby, with showrooms in New York, and their hats were coveted all over the world. Many of them had degrees in costume design and a background in theatre.

Leo and I were met at the front gate by our Mansion concierge, who guided us from the gate entry to the private elevator. On the way we passed a bar called I'll Have Another, named after the 2012 Derby winner who also won the Belmont Stakes. He was heading for the Triple Crown when a tendon injury put him in early retirement at stud. His first foal was named You've Had Enough.

The concierge handed me a glass of champagne to enjoy on the ascent to the sixth floor, and he told Leo he was a beautiful dog. If I needed advice on betting, he would be happy to assist. If I wanted to meet a certain jockey or trainer and their horse, have my picture taken with them, he would set it up, take me there, and use my phone to take the pictures.

Basically, whatever I wanted, he would take care of.

I was not wealthy enough to know what to ask for. I was not wealthy enough to care.

The concierge led us off the elevator and through a hidden door that was manned by tight security. Our concierge smiled, refilled my empty glass of champagne, and ushered us into The Mansion. Leo and I were in the Billionaire's Bunker. We had arrived.

There would be fourteen races today. They began mid-morning and went well into the evening. The Derby itself would run around six PM, give or take.

It was going to be a very long day. But at least I got to wear the hat.

I gave the concierge my phone so he could take a picture of me and Leo. Leo was always photogenic and happy to strike a pose. The crowds were thick, people were happy, noisy, full of energy, and the drinking was already in full swing.

FIFTY

I heard the bugle 'Call to the Post' as my concierge put yet another glass of champagne into my hand. The first race was starting, and like any good Kentucky girl, I was drawn to the bank of windows along the back where I could see the track. Riders had already been called, and the jockeys were maneuvering their horses into the starting gate. Leo put his paws up on the window to get a better view.

'You can't herd them from up here,' I told him.

Behind me the room had the look of a high-end steak house. Stainless steel and marble bars, cushy couches, boxy red dining-room chairs. I had ditched the cane and was sturdy on my feet, walking like a normal human, but my ankle still had a low-level burning ache.

My concierge was back, and he gave me a smile. Did I want another glass of champagne? Something to eat? I shook my head. Did Leo need a bowl of water? I said yes, and he returned with a cut-glass Waterford crystal bowl. He filled it halfway from a shaker of Highbridge Springs water from Kentucky limestone springs. Leo sniffed it and took a drink.

And then I was summoned. A man in a dark charcoal suit that told me he was not here for the fun of it spoke so softly I could not hear him. I had to ask him to repeat.

'Mr Carr would like to invite you to come and have a seat at his table.'

I looked over his shoulder. I had seen pictures of Carr but never seen him in person. A tall man, wide, stooped cadaverous shoulders. Jet-black hair without any gray. Thick dark eyebrows, hooded eyes, an aging face, lined, tired, unfriendly. He wore a seersucker suit and Gucci loafers like half the men in the room.

He stood up at my approach, gave Leo a look of annoyance. I thought I hated him as much as I could hate anyone, but that look at Leo took it up a notch.

'Mrs Lagarde?'

'Sullivan Carr?'

I refused to shake his hand and he studied me just like I studied him. Both of us steeped in mutual dislike.

'I believe you have a video you want to show me.'

He laughed, like I had surprised him. 'Not in a party mood?'

I said nothing. The silence made him uncomfortable.

'I was going to introduce you to—'

'Let's not. If you've met one billionaire, you've met them all. The video. The interview. And then I'll be on my way.'

He didn't like being dictated to. He stared at me a long moment, long enough that we got a few looks.

'Let's sit here, shall we?' I didn't wait for an answer and led him to a horseshoe corner with two blood-red leather armchairs on either side of a small round table.

'I like your hat, Mrs Lagarde.'

'Thank you. I ordered it from Amazon for twenty-seven dollars.'

He gave me a little smile. A waiter brought a box of cigars. Offered them to me first. I didn't turn it down.

'Bring us both a glass of the Screaming Eagle Cabernet.' He raised an eyebrow. 'You like reds, that right? Or would you prefer a bourbon?'

'I don't drink bourbon. But yes, I like reds.'

We lit up and Leo sniffed curiously. The last time I had smoked a cigar was at a jazz club in Knoxville, Tennessee with Olivier. We'd had red wine then too, and split a slice of chocolate torte.

'I understand you have a new Bigfoot logo for VIE. That's a sore point with me. I think you can understand why I might take that personally.'

'And I think you can understand that a sore point with me is the death of three members of my staff. It's time. I want to see the video and I want to see it now.'

He grimaced. 'You know how to take the fun out of things.'

'I think only billionaires think death squads are fun. And you were, after all, one of the major backers in the Torturers' Lobby. Investing in promoting dictators, fascists, and criminals all over the world. So what's one death squad with a background like that?'

'That was a long time ago. There were too many politicians involved. I've moved away from that.'

'And into the destruction of the earth. Yes. You're a busy man.'

'If this is your small talk, I can't wait to hear your questions.'

'The video?'

He reached into his jacket pocket, handed me a cheap burner phone. 'You can keep this. The only thing on this is the video. I had a copy sent to your website an hour ago.'

He leaned back and took a draw on his cigar, and I scrolled the phone until I found what I was looking for.

Madame Reynard again, in her pretty linen dress. The only woman in the room without a hat. I held the phone close, turning up the sound as high as it would go. There was no point turning up the volume on my hearing aids; it would just amplify the ambient noise.

The conversation was not at all what I expected. Madame Reynard was telling him to keep his bitcoin mines in Kentucky, where such things are the norm. That such horrors would not be acceptable in the French Alps, in Chamonix where he liked to ski. And that just fired him up.

He scowled at her. 'What's good enough for Kentucky is good enough for France.'

Madame Reynard had given him an incredulous look. And that was all it took.

One of his buddies across the table offered a million-dollar bet that Carr could not get a bitcoin mine built in the French Alps, and suddenly there was a betting pool between the men at the table, and it was game on. I saw the little smile cross Madame Reynard's face. Everything I thought about the way she did business was right there on the video. Rich influential people playing games with the rest of our lives.

I paused the video. Looked up at Carr who was watching me.

'You built the bitcoin mine on a bet? That is all it was? A bet with your buddies?'

He nodded, laughed hard, cigar smoke streaming out of his nose. 'I know, right? Outrageous. And I collected payment before the French government shut me down.' He grinned at me. 'Keep listening.'

Carr's voice, and that look of mild dislike on Madame Reynard's face. He was talking about VIE. He was talking about me. He was talking about a large sum of money he had forked out for climate change, and why had I not gone along with the game plan? What the hell did I want? If I was trying to soak him for more money with my podcasts and my character assassination, he'd sure as hell see about that.

The next part I knew by heart. The smile on Madame Reynard's face I knew so well.

'You let *me* take care of Junie Lagarde and VIE . . . And, after all, life is getting more and more dangerous for journalists.'

I looked up to see Carr watching me closely. A slow smile spreading across his face.

'This is not proof.'

'No,' he said. 'It's not.'

'And there isn't going to be an interview and you're not going to answer any of my questions.'

'No interview. No questions.'

'But you did do it. You did hire the death squad to come after VIE.'

'Not just VIE. I hired them to come after *you*.'

There was only one reason he would admit this to me. I'd been set up.

'This is The Mansion,' I said. 'You can't get me here.'

'But I can.'

'So you can watch? And did you bet on this too?'

He laughed. 'Guilty as charged. I'd introduce you to my son, but I think the two of you have met.'

'More than once.' I tucked the phone in my purse and stood up.

'He'll find you. He'll find you before you get out of the—'

But then he smiled, looking over his shoulder. 'Oh, there it is.' He glanced back at me. 'My Kentucky Derby blazer, I have a new one made every year. This time it's going to be featured in *Gentlemen's Quarterly*, they're going to send a photographer in for pictures.'

I admit I liked the blazer. Peacock blue with pale cream silk lining, and a pink and gray pocket scarf lapping over the jacket pocket. Sullivan stood up and let the tailor ease him into the jacket, which fit perfectly. The tailor's right hand had a thick fresh white bandage, and I looked up and caught him staring at me.

La Puce.

And I remembered him telling me not to come.

La Puce brushed a bit of nothing off the shoulders of the blazer, jerked it down at the hem and slapped his hand along the back.

Carr gave him a look of annoyance. 'Take it easy, man.'

'Apologies,' La Puce said, slipping away.

I looked back at Sullivan Carr, who grabbed at the back of his jacket, frowning. 'Something's wrong here. Will you get that tailor back?'

'No.' I didn't take orders from billionaires.

I glanced over my shoulder but La Puce had disappeared.

'I . . . what in the hell—' He turned away so I could see his back. 'Can you see anything? I feel like something's moving.'

And then I saw it. A massive snake moving under the lining of the jacket.

'Do you see anything?' I could hear the panic in his voice.

'I do.'

'What the hell is it?'

'Give it a minute. You're about to find out.'

Leo started sniffing and quivering, and I grabbed him and pulled him away.

Sullivan jerked and screamed and blood spurted from his shoulder. He whipped around, and I saw its head rising up out of the collar of the jacket. A timber rattlesnake, and a big one – it would measure on the high end of six feet and was a thick four inches across – and it was working his way across Sullivan Carr's neck and out of the lining of the blazer where it had been sewn in by Les Vipères Emeraudes. A casual cruelty to the snake, and a nightmare for Sullivan Carr.

Leo was attached to my waist by the second leash, and thank God for that. I grabbed both handles on his vest, turned him around and dragged him away, barking and whining. A snake like that would kill him.

I know from The Mansion security camera feeds that we posted on VIE that things went lightning fast, but for me, there in the thick of it . . . the unfolding was slow, a graceful unpredictable dance of death, and I would not need a video to remember it later in every detail which would come to me in dreams, or flash through my mind, sometimes sitting in a cafe drinking coffee, Leo at my feet.

That's when the screaming started. Sullivan Carr. Clawing at his neck and writhing and trying to pull off the Derby blazer as he fell.

'Get it off of me.'

The timber rattler has a high venom yield and long fangs that could go through the material of the coat, and now it had worked its way out, like a second head on Carr's neck. Timber rattle snakes are not aggressive and would prefer to be left alone, but this one was fighting for his life. Carr was bitten eight times, on the neck, the shoulders, the back and the face. Anaphylactic shock kicked in first.

Men and women crowded close, the man in the charcoal suit was nowhere to be seen, and security closed in around Carr as I backed away, keeping a tight hold on Leo who was pulling hard trying to get to Carr.

A man shook his head at me as if I had been naughty. And then I recognized him. Jean-Luc. Head shaved, crisp white shirt, expensive black wool trousers. As promised, I had not seen him coming.

On one level I was aware of the screams, the chaos, but my focus was on the gun that seemed to come out of nowhere and was now securely in the palm of Le Sorcier's hand. He brought it up, aimed straight at me. Tilted his head sideways with a familiar half smile. Then he hesitated.

It was just long enough.

The bullet made him lurch as it went into his back and lodged in his right lung, and he dropped to the floor laying on his side, blood bubbling up on his lips as he mouthed *sorry* before he groaned and his eyes fluttered shut.

Leo lunged, pulling the leash out of my hands, going straight for Sullivan Carr whose screams had faded. And by God, my dog was going back for that snake. I grabbed him and wrestled him down.

I looked up in time to see the man in black, the one who I had seen so many times on the streets of Annecy. He swept off his hat, and bowed very deeply, like he had done so many times before. Thick velvet jacket trimmed in gold, loose breeches and knee-high black boots. For once not smiling beneath the chromed metal mask.

You can get away with that kind of fancy dress at the Derby.

He put a finger to his lips, then disappeared into the crowd.

Carr, no longer moving, flat on a stretcher, was being wheeled out to the elevators. His son, also on a stretcher, blood only barely staunched, went out just behind him, both of them heading for the emergency room at UofL.

Carr's organs began shutting down on the way to the hospital. He was resuscitated and his heart was kept beating and air flowed through his lungs by virtue of the machinery that was always to hand. Coma was followed by renal organ failure and hypotensive shock. Snake bites are not kind to the kidneys. In three days, his organs began deteriorating but the machinery kept him legally alive.

At least he did not know that his horse came third from last, and it was universally agreed that it had been a horrible Derby for Sullivan Carr.

Jean-Luc was still alive.

He had hesitated. I wondered if he would have killed me. I wondered why Les Vipères Emeraudes had saved my life.

Security caught up with me before I could get out of the room, and I huddled in a chair holding tight to Leo. There were going to be questions.

The timber rattler was caught and welcomed with joy by the Louisville Zoo, where timber rattle snakes were cherished. He turned out to be a she, and two months later gave birth to a record fourteen babies.

The humans didn't fare so well.

When Matis wrote a story with the headline *TIMBER RATTLESNAKE SURVIVES BILLIONAIRE ATTACK*, I approved it.

FIFTY-ONE

I was questioned by the head of Churchill Downs security, a man from Texas, in his fifties, intelligent, shrewd. He brought me a bottle of water and a Coke.

'Thought you might like a choice.' His eyes were kind and twinkly.

My hands were shaking, and I hid them under the table where we sat across from each other. Leo was at my feet. Anxious. Standing up when the door opened or closed or the man across from me moved too much in his chair.

'I understand how shook up you must be.'

I nodded. The image was burned into my memory. Le Sorcier – aka Jean-Luc. An assassin, the son of Daddy Sullivan Carr. What was his mother like, I wondered. His mother who had died when he was eight. Because there was a side of him that sure as hell didn't come from his daddy. That side of him that was intelligent, and knowing, and he had gone back and forth with me. Help. Hurt. Follow Daddy's orders.

How close he had come to killing me. A split second and I'd have been gone.

And Sullivan Carr. Luring me there. Setting me up so he could watch me die for a bet.

I knew about bad fathers. Fathers who viewed their children through the lens of obligation, resentment, dislike. Never abusive, never loving, never kind. How much it had affected my brother, Chris; how the assassin had fluctuated, going back and forth, but choosing, in the end, his father. If you save your father's life with the whole world watching, would you not become the number-one son?

'Your brother's here,' the head of security said.

'My brother?'

'You were my sister, I'd be here too. He's polite as can be, but he has let us know that he has called an attorney to help us wrap things up.' He tilted his head. 'But here's the thing. I was right here in the room when you got swarmed by law enforcement, and I think you answered all the questions honestly. But ma'am, I'm not telling you that you are hiding things because you are guilty of anything, but you've been smart enough to answer the questions thrown at you with as little information as possible.

'Now, I'd like to let your brother take you home, or we can have an officer drive you back to your hotel – you said you're staying at the Brown?'

I nodded.

'So, let's clear things up. You've got some history, ma'am. With a group of French terrorists who tried to blow up Mont Blanc.'

I didn't say anything.

'One of the terrorists was from Tennessee.'

I didn't say anything.

'Sad story. But I've got to say this is looking a little hinky. We serve bourbon and I don't like assassinations on the side.'

'You cater to billionaires. They bring trouble. You know that.'

'I know that better than you do. It's been trouble we've handled easily until today. I don't like it.'

'You think I do?'

'You might. I've seen your website.'

I nodded at him. 'Good to know. I hope you read it every day of your life. Get yourself educated.'

He grinned. 'I just might. But you tell me what the hell is going on so I can let you get on out of here.'

He pushed the Coke closer.

I ignored it. Said nothing.

I could have told him about the attack on VIE, and one thing would lead to another with the assassination of my staff, the kidnapping, confinement and protective custody of our journalist Analise Morel, about The Emerald Vipers, a Robin Hood terrorist group that had no trouble both taking out the death squads sent by Daddy Sullivan Carr and forming death squads of their own. Their operatic performance on the Pont des Amours, where they sentenced Sullivan Carr to death, if he did not change his evil ways. Their promise to take down one billionaire a year.

That ought to go down well. That ought to get me in jail really fast. I could see Homeland Security in my future. Or I could keep my mouth shut.

'What business did you have with Carr?'

'I already told you. An interview for VIE.'

'Who bought your ticket today? Who got you invited?'

'Carr did.'
'Why?'
'For the interview. He wanted me to see the kind of life he lived. For our readers to see what kind of life he lived. He was also doing an interview with *Gentlemen's Quarterly*.'
He nodded. 'You understand that threats to billionaires come thick and fast. On the other hand, we haven't lost one yet. Until today.'
'He's dead?'
'If he isn't now, he will be soon. It looks like a hit on Carr and his son.'
'His son?'
'Yes, he was there working security for his dad. You saw him get shot. He was armed but he didn't get his gun out in time. Witnesses saw a man in a mask and a Venetian costume. Do you know who he is?'

So they hadn't seen Jean-Luc try to kill me. I thought about that.

'Mrs Lagarde? Do you know who the man in costume was?'
'No. He was wearing a mask.'
'We'll get him,' he said.

I thought not. But I was smart enough not to say it out loud.

FIFTY-TWO

The attorney sent by my brother arrived just as the questions started all over again. An attorney my brother and I called Sly. Not because it was his name. He came in looking fresh and professional in a gray suit, a pink Oxford shirt, with a conservative gray tie.

Sly looked at me with a bit of a smile.

'I understand you've been interviewing my client for a couple of hours now. I'm here to take her home.'

'I have more questions. It won't take long. You can stay if you like.'

'That's very kind. Mrs Lagarde has had a traumatic day. Is she under arrest? I don't believe you have the authority to put her under arrest, do you?'

He shifted in his seat. 'I do not.'

'That's what I thought. Junie? Shall we go?'

He offered his arm, and I took it.

I wanted to ask questions, but I waited until I got to his car, and he settled both Leo and me into the back seat. My brother was in the front seat, which was something of a surprise.

'Hey, Junie.'

'Hey, Chris.'

'You OK?'

'I'll never be OK again.'

'Did that snake really come up out of Sullivan's Carr's shirt?'

'His blazer. It was sewn into the lining. Like the first *Alien* movie in real life. Where are we going?'

'My house. You're just in time for the rest of my Derby party.'

I leaned back and closed my eyes, wondering if this day would ever end.

'Thanks for getting me out of there so fast, Sly.'

'It's never a good idea to hang around letting them look for probable cause. Even if he was just security. And he didn't have the authority to keep you there. Next time, just leave.'

'How long before I can go home to France?'

'How does it stand with the police?'

'I made a witness statement.'

'You're not under arrest. You made a statement. No reason you can't go home.'

'So, I can go?'

'You can.' Then he gave me a sideways smile. 'If it were me, I'd be thinking the sooner the better.'

FIFTY-THREE

Practically speaking, Sullivan Carr died before he made it to the University of Louisville Hospital ER.
 Clinically dead, but not legally dead. Digestive failure. Kidney failure. Heart failure. Kept alive by life support.
 To his credit, Sullivan Carr had not chosen the route of billionaires who are sure they can beat death. Who choose to be infused with what is basically antifreeze and placed under liquid nitrogen in a vat large enough to hold up to four 'whole-body patients' and five 'neuropatients,' which was their term for head only. They could float there until the end of time, on the off chance that revival would one day become possible. Whether their families visited them in the vats was something I did not want to know.
 Their money was kept safe in a cryonic suspension trust, because the notion that 'you can't take it with you' does not apply to billionaires.
 Carr, conservative from birth, had instead routed his assets into a dead-hand trust, in which the wealth protection industry had recently pushed through legislation to change the 99-year cap to five hundred years. His estate had been set up so money flowed to his family as long as he was alive – so alive he would be.
 Whether or not Sullivan Carr had any awareness is hard to know. But if he did, then day in and day out he would listen to the whine of machinery. Twenty-four hours a day without a break. A lot like living next to a bitcoin mine.

FIFTY-FOUR

When Sly pulled into Chris's driveway, Chris got out first and opened the passenger door to let Leo out. 'Hello, you handsome animal, where they hell have you been? Why are they keeping you in France?'

Chris looked good. Crisp khaki pants. Expensive Egyptian white shirt. Expensive loafers. Low key. Comfortable. He was not the kind of man to wear a green plaid bow tie, and yet here he was, wearing one.

'I see Leo is not the only dude in a handsome bow tie.'

'You are always in some kind of trouble, Junie. I bet you keep that French husband of yours run off his feet.'

'I'm worth it.'

He enveloped me in a long, hard hug. 'Hey, Junie, I looked at your website. VIE. Always the overachieving little sister. I might be proud.' He gave me a sideways smile. 'Come on in the house.'

And what a house it was.

My brother and I had opposite tastes in architecture. It was a sixties classic, mid-century modern A-frame. You were not going to find my brother in Old Louisville, which has the largest Victorian neighborhood in the country. He had no interest in the Highlands, where people with money like to live. He had settled in Greenleaves on one and a half wooded acres, and his house had so many big windows you felt like you lived in the woods. I loved the great room – vaulted ceiling and a floor-to-ceiling double-sided stone fireplace which had sold my brother on the house the moment he'd seen it. Knotty pine walls and hardwood floors reminded me of our grandmother's house in Danville. Leo loved it here, running through the woods out back. Looking through the windows at the squirrels. Laying outside on the deck. A perfect place for a Derby party. A perfect place for Chris and Redmond. The house was hidden behind bushes and trees, the driveway crushed gravel and grass, and it was like living in a giant treehouse.

'Oh, and Junie. Gatsby's here.'

'Then I'm leaving.'

'He needs to talk to you.'

'I do not want to see that fucking Gatsby ever again, Chris, much less talk to him.'

'Nevertheless, you will. You have to. Trust me, Junie. You do.'

I glared at him. 'I won't promise to be nice.'

'Goes without saying.'

Gatsby was cross-legged on the floor of my brother's living room drinking Maker's Mark bourbon straight out of a bottle and absolutely coming unglued. To be fair he was not so bad looking, but aging at an accelerated rate, with lines of dissolution and plastic surgery blurring his face.

He expressed bewilderment.

Anger that things had turned out so badly for him and his father and his brother.

He asked me to explain a dead hand trust.

I ignored him and dragged an ottoman in front of an armchair, took my boots off, and settled in.

Chris looked around the living room. 'Where did everybody go?'

His husband, Redmond, came in from the kitchen. 'I sent them home, Chris, I did not think your sister would like a crowd after what happened this afternoon.' He turned to me. 'I am so glad you are OK, Junie. You have had a terrible day. I made you a dirty martini. Chris told me once that you liked them.'

'Thank you, Redmond. I haven't had one in three years.'

'Don't they have dirty martinis in France?' Chris asked.

'I've never asked.'

So often I think I am alone in the world. But truly, I'm not. Though on days like this, I might prefer it.

'I know you stole my horse.' Gatsby glared at me, then put his head in his hands.

'She was mine to steal.'

'So you admit it?'

I looked at Chris, who shrugged. 'He's not that smart sober. Drunk, you aren't going to get any sense out of him. But Gatsby has brought you some paperwork that his brother took from your house, though how he tracked it down in your attic is a mystery to me.

'If it's paperwork, Chris, it was in the file cabinet.'

'I guess that explains it. Hand it over, Gatsby, and tell her you're sorry, or she'll put you on her website and tomorrow you'll be a meme.'

Gatsby looked up. 'Please don't put me on your website.' He handed me a file. The paperwork on Empress. Her National Show Horse registration. Her bill of sale.

'Jean-Luc took that out of my house? Son of a bitch.'

'Don't talk like that about my brother; he's dead. He was my big brother and I loved him and I looked up to him. I've also got the phones he told me to hang on to. We were going to keep them in case we ever had trouble with my dad.'

'He's not dead,' Chris said. 'He was still hanging on, last I heard.'

'Oh. That's good news.'

'Where are the phones?' I asked him.

'In the car. But I don't think I should drive.'

'No, you shouldn't drive, Gatsby,' Chris said, slapping him on the back. 'Looks like Sly is heading out the door. Sly, you want to run Gatsby home on your way out?'

Sly rubbed the back of his neck. 'Don't think I won't bill you for that.'

'Hey, Gatsby,' Chris said, walking him toward the door. 'I've got a safe here in my office if you need a good place to keep those phones safe. Probably shouldn't keep them in your car.'

FIFTY-FIVE

The brown padded envelope that Gatsby had given my brother to keep safe held two burner phones and the emerald of death that Sullivan Carr had gotten from the Vipers. Wrapped exactly like mine.

Redmond, Chris and I watched the videos from the attack on VIE at the kitchen table. I put the martini down without tasting it.

We had our proof. I had gotten what I came for.

'Junie,' my brother said as I headed out the door.

'I need a little time to myself.'

I saw a kaleidoscope of images as I walked backward through time, colors, noise, faces. Frozen moments. Flashes of light.

I had been there for the aftermath, and at last I saw it unfold, starting at the beginning now, knowing exactly what was going to come next.

I latched onto moments, my mind grabbing hold of the images of Clementine. Valiant, courageous, black knit cap on her head as it always was, rushing into gunfire with wide-open arms and her dark hair streaming out behind her as she screamed, '*Courez. Sauvez-vous.*' Run. Save yourselves. Then a glimpse of open balcony doors, and papers blowing off a desk. Gunfire and the swirl of wind.

Louis shouting out, 'Ah, les bâtards' – you bastards – as he spins sideways and drops, and a slam from the kitchen as the camera pans to Timothée looking lethal with the paring knife in his fist. Then down he goes, falling sideways, a look of acceptance on his face as if *game over* is his final thought.

Already the memories were fading as I walked through the woods with Leo. Already the woods and my dog and the breeze in my hair worked to gently push the images away, as if my mind would no longer hold them.

And then it would start again, a series of disconnected moments going off like fireworks in my memory.

Stéphane blocking the bathroom door where Analise hides. La Puce looming suddenly in the shadows of the tight hallway. The camera falling and the lens washed in blood. A glimpse of a limp hand still wrapped around a gun.

And I am there. In the front office, turning to the kitchen. I hear it again. *Recording the death of Junie Lagarde* . . .

The next sequence comes as a freeze-frame jumble of moments, in no particular order. A cup of coffee splattered on the floor. A backpack under a desk. A chair gone sideways.

I stop a moment and just breathe. Then I am going forward again, Leo padding along beside me, with a small branch in his mouth, carrying it through the woods at the back of my brother's house. We have been walking a while. I told myself I was in Kentucky, that all of this was over, and the well-worn path of hard packed dirt felt familiar and eased me along. I was aware of how the light filtered through the trees, the soft sound of the wind, of my footsteps on the path.

There was a tree I was heading for. A black walnut that was there before I was born and would still be there long after I was gone.

'Here,' I told Leo, as I settled to the ground, back to the tree that felt like solid comfort against my shoulders. Leo settled beside me, stretched out, chewing on the branch he had been carrying. Dogs chew to process stress. I lean against a tree.

I tilted my head back, one leg outstretched, one knee up, closed my eyes, and crumbled leaves in my hand.

It was good to be in Kentucky. It was good to be in the woods with my back against a tree. It was good to have my dog.

I had watched the video expecting horror, and found instead the last glimpses of beautiful lives, and I was glad to have witnessed it, with peculiar curious dread, afraid of what I would see, my hands in fists. To be there and live it with them, to watch with love and flat-out admiration, because it was all I *could* do . . . and all they would have asked of me. So young. Warriors.

And now I wanted to sleep. Lean against the tree with Leo and stay in the woods forever.

Sullivan Carr was on death support; Le Sorcier was finding his way back to life in intensive care, and VIE was thriving, stronger than ever, powerful with the voices of people who watched and reported back, who found the agency to make small changes where they could, all of us part of something that was growing. Growing.

And somewhere in Annecy the swans glided through the canals, and the streets were full of people, walking, biking, dogs on leashes, and I wondered if Les Vipères Emeraudes were still sliding through the crowds, masked and mysterious. I wondered where the man in black was now. The man who had saved my life.

But I was tired. Right down to my soul.

I was here, back against a tree, in the only place I could be at ease, and away from the world. I would not go home. *This* was home. These woods. This tree. This dog. I shut my eyes tight and refused to think of anything else. I pictured myself right where I was, never leaving, always sleeping, leaves blowing over me, snow, rain, sunshine. None of it mattered as long as I could sleep. I had done my best. I was slipping away.

And then my brother's voice. Murmuring to Redmond, the two of them noisy on the path.

'There she is.'

I heard them stop. Felt their presence just a few feet away. Leo jumping up and whimpering with happiness. I kept my eyes shut tight. Eventually they would go away. I wasn't ever going to leave.

'Come on, Junie, let's get back to the house.'

'*No.*'

'Yeah, but come on. It's getting dark.'

'How did you know where to find me?'

My brother laughed, and I opened my eyes. I was annoyed. I did not want to wake up.

'It's where you always are. Don't you remember? Redmond, my sister used to run away from first grade, like clockwork, every week. She'd wait for everybody to line up for lunch, then bolt out the back door, and run like hell fire down the slope at the edge of the parking lot. Her teacher could never catch her or even follow because she wore high pointy heels, and she'd scream, "Come back now, young lady, get yourself back up here right this minute."'

Redmond leaned down. He offered me a hand and I took it, brushing leaves off my sweater, wishing they had let me be.

'You did not like school?' he asked gently.

'I had a lot of questions they wouldn't answer. At least not to my satisfaction.'

He gave me a sideways look. 'How old were you then?'

Chris laughed. 'She was *six*. And they would come and get me out of my classroom and send me off to find her. And I knew where she'd be. Down that slope and into the woods, and when I asked her where she thought she was going, she'd say the same thing every time.'

I smiled at my brother. 'Off to seek my fortune in the world.'

FIFTY-SIX

Leo and I were up early the next morning, and I wanted to hit the road, go home, close up the house. I had snagged the first flight we could get out of Cincinnati and we would endure a long layover in Dulles so we could get home.

My brother did not get up until noon on the weekends, and sometimes the weekdays, so I drank coffee in the kitchen. I didn't want to leave without telling him goodbye. But he wandered in earlier than expected, barefooted, wearing old jeans and a tee-shirt.

'You want to stay for a while, Junie?'

I shook my head. 'No, I need to get home.'

'You talk to your husband?'

'His name is Philippe. In case you forgot.'

'Not sure you ever told me.'

'Yeah we talked off and on all night. He can't decide if he's mad at me or just happy I'm alive. If I don't go home, he'll come here. I'm booked on a flight out tomorrow morning.'

He sat down at the table. 'I know I wasn't great to you when Olivier died.'

'Nobody's great at a time like that.'

'We're good?'

'We're good.'

'How did you like The Mansion?'

'It was nice, but it didn't feel like a horse race. I like to be out in the stands where I can see the horses run.'

'OK. Well. Next time you want to have a shootout at Churchill Downs, I'm your guy.'

It was strange going back to the cottage. Leo ran wild in the backyard while I got packed and the house tucked away. I had been all set to sell it, but now I wasn't sure. It was OK not to know. I would just sit with that until I did. I wanted to spend time here with Philippe. Take him out for barbecue, sit with him on the porch swing. Nothing special is what I liked best. I was feeling homesick for Kentucky. I wanted to spend some time with my brother. I wanted to see a movie in English.

But for now, what I wanted was to be home in France with Philippe.

FIFTY-SEVEN

Philippe was waiting for us at the Geneva airport when Leo and I walked down to the bottom level for baggage, taxis, and an exit. He was waiting quietly to one side, smiling at me, steady and patient as always. Leo barked when he saw him, and I wrapped my arms around him. It was an easy thirty-five minute drive to our apartment in Annecy, and I could barely wait to get back home to France.

'You are glad to be home?' he asked me.

'Very.'

'I have news of Le Sorcier.'

I looked away. 'Dead?'

'Just the opposite. He has left the hospital. Gatsby hired him an expensive lawyer with a strange name.'

'Sly?'

'Yes, you know him?'

I laughed. 'Yeah, he's pretty great.'

'Evidently there was nothing to charge him with. Nobody saw him do anything; everybody was watching Sullivan Carr wrestle the snake. But Sly thought he should leave Lexington as soon as he was able, and not be in a hospital where law enforcement could get a hand on him. *Don't make it easy*, is what he advised. Does that upset you?'

'No. I'm glad.'

'Why?'

'I have no idea.'

He carried my bag and my purse and I just had to hold Leo's leash.

'Philippe? Where did you get your information on this?'

He shrugged. Smiled. 'Your brother called. He thought you'd want to know.'

'At least now I should be safe at Monoprix.'

FIFTY-EIGHT

Late the next day, on a quiet Sunday afternoon, I went to the VIE office to get some work done on my own. I was the only one who ever went there on the weekend.

I found Madame Reynard waiting for me in my office, which I had left locked up with the alarm on. I gave her a hard look, masking the fleeting moment of shock. It was not that she had been able to find her way in. It was that she'd left her lair in Metz yet again to meet with me. That couldn't be good.

She wore a beautifully cut black blazer and large white pearl earrings that caught my eye and stirred a bit of envy. Her glorious hair was piled on her head with the abandon of someone who takes it for granted that she is fabulous. Beautiful women who try to kill you are annoying.

In an astonishingly rude power play, she was sitting behind my desk. A very large desk that would never fit into my apartment, a vintage and quite battered Chippendale – a classic style bringing a touch of elegance and distinction, beneath my usual mess.

Evidently, she liked my desk too. I could see that she had taken a moment to rifle through the stack of papers, the notepads, no doubt had gone through the drawers. She held up a disposable fountain pen.

'Why don't you splurge and buy something nice?'

'I have, many times. I always lose them. It is odd how the cheap ones are easier to keep track of, but maybe it's just that I don't notice when they're gone.'

She tilted her head and gave me the bland smile, instead of the mean one. As far as I know she only has two, but she is a woman of endless talent.

'I would offer you a coffee, but it looks like you already have one.' I turned my back on her because I had Leo to keep an eye out. I unhooked his leash. 'Go to work.'

He stayed on his feet for a long moment, looking her over.

'Does he want me to pet him?' she asked.

'No. He doesn't like to be petted by strangers any more than I do.'

She had the perplexed expression of a woman who does not get animals. 'You are saying that there are dogs who don't want to be petted?'

'Why are you here?' I asked her.

Leo settled into one of two well-worn cognac leather armchairs in front of the balcony windows, keeping an eye on both of us. I went into the kitchen.

'I made a full pot, Junie; do help yourself.'

I poured myself a cup, put in a generous splash of heavy whipping cream, and settled next to Leo in the second leather armchair. We usually sat side by side in the end-of-week VIE meeting, which my staff found hilarious. Most of them favored high-tech chairs with complicated settings, metal tubing, and small scoop-shaped seats.

'I quite like this coffee maker of yours. American?'

'Dutch. Not everyone has to have a Nespresso.'

She tilted her head to one side, studying me. I would say she was more than usually unhappy with me.

'Why are you here? Why do you just keep showing up, every time I turn around?'

'I will never like you, Junie. You are also more annoying than anyone I know, and I know a lot of difficult people. It is the nature of my job.'

'Tragic for you. And you can call me Madame Lagarde.'

'I have had an unpleasant visit with Philippe.'

'Ah. My husband.'

'He has handed me a certain digital file of information and let me know that everything on the file has been given to you. I assume you have this information?'

I smiled.

'You've got it backwards. All the information came from VIE. I shared it with him, that's all.' I tilted my head sideways. I look cute when I do that. Philippe especially finds it attractive. 'I have already published the information that you're the one who encouraged Daddy Sullivan Carr to build the bitcoin mine, in a historic location in the Alps, as a lure to trash his reputation and push legislation that would bring him to the notice of the world, infuriate him, and crush his dark but egotistical little heart, as he was showered with bad publicity. Being rich, it never occurred to him he could not have what you told him he wanted. I have published proof that Sullivan Carr sent the death squads to VIE. So again . . . why are you here? There is nothing you need from me. Somehow you are not destroyed by all of this. You are still beloved by the government. Are you just here to gloat?'

She frowned. 'I do not love that word, but it is true. I am here to gloat. All of your hard work, and your speeches with Analise Morel, your podcasts, the little songs you play, your Bigfoot eating baguettes. You prove what billionaires and I myself are up to and nothing changes. It is hopeless. Give up.'

'For every one of you we get rid of, three more will take your place.'

'And so you admit it is hopeless?'

'How so? Everybody is still going about their regular lives, raising kids, going to work, walking and feeding their dog, just normal stuff. And the results have been stellar. A bitcoin mine is shut down. Sullivan Carr is not only out of business, he is technically if not legally dead. Nobody expects people like you to be held accountable by the rule of law, or regulations, since the game is fixed. You're like bad weather. You live in a bubble and nobody cares. We have no more plans for articles or podcasts about you or Sullivan Carr. Your think tanks, your symposiums, your media pundits and editorials are only read by people like you. The rest of us don't give a shit.'

'Are you trying to tell me I'm not relevant?'

'That's the word I was looking for.'

She gave me a look of pure dislike.

'And if I offer you the bribe again? This time with a paper trail for proof and no strings attached?'

'I'll turn you down. And bribes are old news. Nobody much cares about that either.'

'Be honest, Junie. Don't you walk past the beautiful apartments on Rue Josef Blanc and every single day wish you could live there?'

'No,' I told her. 'It's more like twice a week.'

'I don't understand you, Junie.'

'Just be content with not liking me.'

I walked her to the doorway, Leo keeping an eye on both of us as he had from the moment she'd arrived. She hesitated and tilted her head to one side. 'You are saying we live in two worlds. Are you saying my world does not affect yours?'

'Just the opposite. But what you keep losing sight of is that my world affects yours too. And there are more of us than there are of you.'

'You are envious, I think, Madame Junie Lagarde. Very middle class, in the USA. State college, a little life in the south, growing up in the suburbs with your mother, your father, your brother. No elite schools, no big houses, no trips to Europe when you were a little girl. No brand-new car for your sixteenth birthday. Your bourgeois hatred for people better than you, people with money to burn, all the things they have that you cannot have. That is why you are doing this. Envy and revenge.'

'Richer than me, not better. And you're half right. Envy, no. I love my little life, I love my family, my husband, my dog, my small apartment over a restaurant, my little Kentucky cottage downtown. I don't want your life; I don't want their life; I want my life and my life only. But revenge? Oh, you bet. *That* is what I want. And you are the ones with envy. You are the ones whose lives are never enough, who look at people like me and can't stand it, because whatever we have, you want that too.

'And in a world full of media that is controlled by the wealthy and the privileged, where we have lost the thread of what is real and what is fake, what is generated by the blatant, jumbled intellectual theft of AI, what is pure spin and manipulation . . . in a world where there isn't any truth or any trust . . . there is VIE. No spin, no lies, just honesty, as far as we can take it, and knowledge. It's power for the little people like me. And this tiny bit of power scares you and it scares them – and it should. Some day, somehow, some way . . . we're going to take you bastards down.'

FIFTY-NINE

Three nights later Les Vipères Emeraudes came for me. I had thought it was over. I was wrong.
Philippe and I had planned to meet at Brasserie du Théâtre. It was late, uncrowded, and I was sitting outside at a table for two, waiting. I had gone from the barn to the office and then to the restaurant and did not have Leo. I wasn't sure if that made it better or worse.

When I saw the man in black coming up the street, his chromed metal mask glinting in the moonlight, I knew he was coming for me. Philippe was on the way. There were waiters close by. Better to stay where I was.

He sat down at my table, silent as always.

My hands began to shake. 'Monsieur, I am waiting for my husband. He may be late, but he'll be here. I ask you to leave immediately.'

The man cocked his head to one side. 'I think your husband is exactly on time.'

And then I understood.

I knew that voice, though it took a minute for me to catch my breath. Philippe waited patiently with a slow smile.

'How many times have you done this, Philippe?'

'Many times. I am sorry I frightened you. That was not my intent.'

'What was your intent?'

'To watch over you. To protect you. To blow off the head of the man who tried to assassinate you at the Kentucky Derby.'

'That was you, Philippe? At the Derby? You shot Le Sorcier?'

He took the cloth napkin and wiped the tears off my cheeks. 'Do you think, madame, that I will let ones such as that stalk you and make you afraid?' His voice was very hard. 'Do you think I will sleep easy in my bed when I know they will come for you? Do you think there is anything I won't do to keep you safe?'

'So when was it you and when was it them?'

'So often it was both, madame. When they were stalking you, I would follow them. And why, Junie, did you not tell me when you got the emerald?'

I looked away. 'I don't know. Everything was such a mess.'

'Is it because you had decided to go to the Derby and did not want to tell me about that?'

'Maybe. I don't know. Honestly – yes.'

He nodded. 'I have been infiltrating the meetings of these vipers, and I know who some of them are. Which is a knowledge that will be dangerous to the both of us, and that I can use to keep us safe. They ask that I leave them alone and not expose them, and I tell them I will kill them if they come close to my wife in any way other than to protect you, and we now have an understanding. La Puce knows this. They will factor this in. They are not to be trusted, but they have never done anything but watch over you, madame.'

And La Puce had brought me my horse.

'How did you figure out that I had gotten the emerald?'

'Junie, you left it in the kitchen drawer.'

'Let's sell it. Do you think it's worth much? What do emeralds go for?'

He gave me a smile. 'Emeralds do not go for so much, and selling it will not be possible, I regret that the emerald has been crushed.'

'Crushed? How do you crush an emerald?'

'It is actually not a difficult thing; they are brittle like bones. I used the mallet Eugene left when he was repairing the kitchen floor. I picked it up on my way out the door, and it turned out to be exactly right for the occasion.'

The power-nail white mallet. I felt a little queasy. Looked again at my husband. The same man I had gone to bed with last night and woken up with this morning.

'Exactly right for what? What did you do, Philippe?'

'I had a short visit with La Puce the night I found the emerald in the drawer. I took it to him and said I had come to return it and there were things for us to discuss. I did not like that he knew it had been delivered and did not tell me.

'He told me that the emerald did not come from the Vipers. That Sullivan Carr sent it. To make you afraid, to make you suspicious, to ruin the uneasy alliance you had with Les Vipères. To make sure you went to the Derby to meet with him. I offered La Puce the emerald, and when he reached for it, I put it into the palm of his hand and then used the mallet to crush both. And then I asked him again if there was anything else that I should know.'

'Philippe.'

He shrugged. 'That is when he told me you should not go to the Derby because Carr was setting you up to be killed. And to be fair, he did tell you not to go. And he assured me Sullivan Carr would die. And I took him after to the emergency room.'

'I saw the bandage on his hand. So that was you?'

'Let us say that his ability as a marksman is now a thing of the past. I understand he is training with his other hand.'

'But why did Le Sorcier get an emerald? He told me the Vipers sent one to him too, the same day I got one. I thought they were . . .' I trailed off.

'No one sent an emerald to Le Sorcier, my love. He would know his father sent one to you, to frighten you, so that you would not trust them. If he says he gets one too, that makes you think they do not want you to talk to Carr because he can prove he did not send the death squads.'

'Which I have now proved he did.' I closed my eyes tight. 'And I fell for it.'

He reached across the table and took my hand. It was as if I were seeing a stranger, in the face of my husband. It was thrilling and it made me worry. What else did I not know about him?

He ordered wine, and it came discreetly, and he filled my glass. 'We have not trusted each other well lately, have we, my wife? I understand now what it is you have been so angry about, how the deception comes between us. It becomes a triangle, does it not? You on one point, me on one point, and the lie on the other. So now it all makes sense to me. I can only tell you that I was worried for my son. The divorce was very hard for all of us. And this was a moment of resentment from him, and I didn't want to call him on it. But I did not have to. That was not what you asked for. You asked for me to be honest with you, to be together on this. But instead I lied to you, because it was easy. Because I did not have to face the rudeness of my son. And in doing that I betrayed you. At the time it seemed like such a small thing, better forgotten. But it was the beginning of the mess we have made. Can we promise each other that we will fight this? And have a core of honesty between the two of us, as much as is possible in a complicated world? Because you and I, we have enemies now. We need each other to survive. We must never let anyone or anything get between us again.'

I squeezed his hand. Nodded. Took a sip of wine and laughed. 'I'm surprised we didn't cross paths at the airport.'

'No, I was on a late flight out after the Derby. I was out of the US before you even made reservations to get back to France. But the day before the Derby, I was there. I drove past the little cottage of yours and I wanted to knock on the door, build a fire in the fireplace outside, and throw balls to Leo in the yard. This home in Kentucky calls to me somehow. As if I have been happy there before.'

I met his eyes. The way he looked at me, so intensely, but with a hint of mischief in his smile.

'It's your cottage too. I was thinking to sell it.'

'Let's plan a trip, take Leo to run in his backyard. I will take August off.'

'Oh, God, August in Kentucky? No. We'll go in October, and I will take you to the races at Keeneland, can you make time for that?'

He smiled. 'Bien sûr. But we will also go in August when all of France, including me, is on holiday. Madame, you cannot change the habits of an entire country. But we will go in October too. I want to eat barbecue, and sit in front of the fireplace with a cognac; I want to try bourbon, and go with you on your favorite drive on Old Frankfort Pike. I also want to go and hike in the Smoky Mountains, it is close, is it not?'

'A three-hour drive.'

'We will avoid the bears when we hike. Also – I would like to meet our horse.'

'I'll take you to meet her tomorrow.'

He studied me for a long moment. Then took my hand. 'Do you remember dancing with me that night in your kitchen, as we were falling in love? And I seduced you so well.'

'I remember.'

He smiled at me in a way that brought a thrill. 'Tonight you will dance with the Black Marquis. And tonight you will not be afraid.'

SIXTY

The very next morning, I took Philippe to the barn to meet Empress. He did not disappoint. His gentleness won her heart, and the two of us walked her on a soft lead rope down a worn dirt road, my ankle strong and stable. We rambled slowly through the gentle valley slopes, letting Empress stop to graze whenever she wanted, which meant we spent a lot of time standing still. And I knew that my horse was very happy.

I squeezed Philippe's hand. 'Why did you do it, Philippe? The mask and the costume, never telling me it was you.'

'Mainly to watch over you. As a Venetian, I could blend in and keep an eye on you while the Vipers were doing the same, which I did not like. But they do not know I am not one of them, so it gives me much freedom. And also.' He gave me a sideways look. 'I want to seduce you a bit. To be a handsome, mysterious protector in your life when you and I . . . we are having such distance between us. I am a stranger; you are a married woman. But it is OK I think to hand you a bouquet. But it went wrong because it became clear that it made you afraid. Even with Leo beside you. And while the goal was to use this as a way to watch over you with the Vipers unaware, I didn't like that it made you more afraid.'

'Men don't see danger the way women do.'

'Next time I will wear a mask and nothing else, so you will know it is me.'

And that night, when we curled up together in bed, Philippe smiled at me and said the one thing I had been wanting to hear.

'You were right, madame. I lied to you. Children in France do not eat Oreo cookies for breakfast. And now I will make love to you. Say that you want me to.'

'I want you to.'

But afterwards, as I drifted between waking and sleep, I wondered what else I did not know about my husband. What else did he not know about me. How much do we know about anyone, really, as we stand together on the sidelines, or get caught up.

But then I remembered him. All of the things we had lived through together, the intense and the mundane. If I knew nothing else, I knew his heart.

And I saw in Philippe everything that I loved, born of the time we had spent together, in this lifetime and in others, that certain smile he had, the strength of his hand on mine, the lines of life experience on his intelligent face – all of this made him ever more beautiful to me. I decided not to worry about the way things would unfold around us in the moment, in the future or the past. We had the now of the dreamworld, and the real that awaits.